ON THE ROCKS

LOVE AFTER MIDNIGHT #3

ELISE FABER

SNARKY BOOKS FOR SNARKY MINDS

ON THE ROCKS
BY ELISE FABER

ON THE ROCKS
Copyright © 2020 Elise Faber
Print ISBN-13: 978-1-946140-80-7
Ebook ISBN-13: 978-1-946140-79-1
Cover Art by Jena Brignola

LOVE AFTER MIDNIGHT

Rum And Notes

Virgin Daiquiri

On The Rocks

Sex On The Seats

ONE

Anabelle

I SLIPPED out the front door of my friend Iris's house, several containers of leftovers balanced in my hands, and struggled to close it behind me.

The Christmas party inside was still going strong, but I had to head out. The only plus in having to leave early was that at least I was able to bring treats with me—albeit more of them than was polite. Still, I didn't have any shame. Iris had offered—she was a brilliant baker—and I had accepted. Easy as that. Now, I was taking my stash to my car—the one I'd finally been able to afford to buy, in part because of the crew inside this little house.

My boss and the owner of Bobby's, the bar where I worked, Kace.

My coworker, Brent, who was charming, even with the most annoying of customers.

Their women—Brooke and Iris. Though maybe it would be more accurate to say that Kace and Brent were *their* men.

Because those men no longer held their own hearts. They'd trusted them to Brooke and Iris's safekeeping.

It was great. I was happy for them.

But also . . . it wasn't for me.

I wasn't looking for a happy ending. I just wanted a safe place. I wanted to make a living and not rely on anyone else. I wanted to control my temper so I didn't dump a Cosmopolitan in the lap of a handsy customer and instead carefully dissuaded him from being an asshole.

Okay, that last one was a lie.

I definitely didn't mind dumping cocktails on handsy fucking customers, especially when those customers had an open tab I could charge said cocktail to.

I kind of liked being an asshole.

Just slightly less than I liked the crew inside. So, I wasn't looking for an exit, an escape from the love and the happily ever afters inside. Rather, I'd offered to go in and meet the alcohol delivery at Bobby's the next morning, to save the lovebirds from an early morning.

Which meant it was time for me to go.

I fumbled with the knob, shifting the containers to grab it. When that failed, I lifted a foot and tried to use *that* to close the door.

Newsflash. I wasn't a member of Cirque de Soleil, so it didn't work.

Sighing, I bent to place the containers down, something I should have just done in the first place.

Always trying to take the easy way out, Ana Girl. Sometimes it's better to just take the hard one from the beginning.

"Thanks, Mom," I muttered under my breath.

Ten years gone and still chastising me from the wrong side of the grave.

Still never failed to make me smile.

She would like my friends.

"Don't."

I stopped mid-bend at the male voice.

"I've got it."

Tall. *Really* tall. Dark hair with a reddish tint. Olive skin. Bright blue eyes. And, *oh NBD*, maybe also the most handsome man I'd ever met.

I swallowed hard then frowned when he reached past me to close the door.

Then frowned harder when he rang the doorbell.

"Um," I began, wanting to ask him what in the ever-loving-fuck he was doing. But the doorbell had been rung and footsteps approached, and the wooden panel swung back open to reveal Brooke standing on the threshold, smile wide. "Did you forget something, An . . . a . . . *belle?*"

The smile faded from Brooke's face.

Her olive skin went pale.

Her eyes widened. Her eyes . . . that were the same shape as those of the man towering over me on the porch.

Kace came up behind her. "Everything okay—"

Brooke didn't answer him, just reached a hand out as though she expected to encounter a ghost, her voice shaking when she spoke.

"Hayden?"

TWO

Hayden

I DIDN'T KNOW why I expected this to be easy.

Seeing my sister's face pale, tears fill her green eyes, her mouth agape.

She wavered on her feet but before I could reach her, before I could catch her like I had caught her so many times before— my younger-by-ten-minutes sister, my shadow, the girl who had been mine more than she'd been my parents—before I could close the distance, a muscled arm slid around her middle.

A muscled *male* arm.

With tattoos.

Of course, *I* had tattoos, but that wasn't the point. This was my sister, my baby sister, and no man would be good enough, least of all a tattooed, pretty boy who was scowling down at me.

I'd seen this man in pictures. Kissing her. Touching her.

I'd wanted to kill him then. Had only refrained because I could tell, even through photographs, that my sister was happy.

Now, seeing his hands on her, the confident, familiar hold,

and I wanted to pull out the gun strapped into my holster and threaten this man within an inch of his life.

And *then* kill him anyway.

"Brooke?" he whispered. "Are you—?"

"Holy fucking shit," Brent said. He had been my unit commander, but we were more like brothers. Close enough that it had been as difficult keeping my secrets from him as they had been to keep from Brooke. "Hayden—" A sharp shake of his head. "I—"

Movement from my right, from the tiny, curved beauty who barely made it up to my chest. "Okay, clearly there is more going on here than I'm following," she said, her voice soft on the surface, although I could sense the strength beneath. "Let's take this off the porch and figure it out inside." Her eyes, deep pools of hickory, flicked toward me and the soft flecked away to reveal the steel underneath. "You. Stay here."

"Ana—" Brooke began.

"Stay," that steel said, not letting her finish, "means to stay on this fucking porch. It does not mean you get to disappear, and it does not mean to come in unless you're invited. Got it?"

I had to bite back a grin.

She was protective, this Anabelle, and I, for one, approved. I also approved of the lusciousness of her five-foot-nothing body, but then again, I'd never been a man who liked a rail-thin woman.

Curves.

All day, every day.

And Anabelle had them—

She cleared her throat, eyes narrowing, and I nodded. Because her curves were so not the point.

Brooke was the point. Brent was the point.

I'd been gone too long. I was tired. I wanted . . . my family again.

Anabelle glared at me for one more minute before setting down the containers she'd been fumbling with when I'd walked onto the porch—the reason I'd first noticed her curves, had found my motion stilled on the driveway as I'd watched her contort herself in her attempts to close the door without setting anything down.

Amused. Aroused.

Neither emotion had been in the forefront of my mind in the last few years. Not since—

I blinked, shoved that all down, and kept my expression placid as the door shut.

Then again, I'd had plenty of practice with that as well.

Shutting out the things I cared about. Pretending they didn't exist.

But it was done.

I was out.

Finally.

I listened through the closed door as the volume of voices increased, male and female voices overlapping, becoming a muffled vibration that told me the conversation wasn't going to end any time soon.

My gaze drifted to the plastic containers of food, and my stomach rumbled.

I was hungry, had skipped eating in favor of finally seeing my sister . . . and I knew she was going to be supremely pissed when she found out I'd been keeping tabs on her even as I'd pretended to be dead in order to . . . *shit*. None of my reasons seemed worth it now.

And Brent—

Fuck. I hadn't missed the betrayal in his eyes.

Not a hint, not inching in on the edges. It was there. Full-force.

"Shit," I muttered, aloud this time. Ten years ago, I hadn't felt like I had a choice. I'd needed to do what I did, and the explosion, the subsequent injuries to me, the team, to Brent, had provided the cover I'd needed to slip away.

Let them think I was dead.

It was easier that way.

Because it was more than likely that I would end up that way anyway.

Instead . . . here I was.

I shifted, my knee that had been injured in the explosion, which had taken several of my friends and injured Brent severely, aching from the long flight.

Left with an aching knee when my friends had died.

That was all the perspective I needed.

All the perspective I needed to shove the memories out of my brain—also injured in the blast, though I'd recovered from that, too. So long as I didn't pay attention too closely to the dreams that sometimes came on fast and furious, stealing my breath, putting me back into that place, making me remember the chaos and fear and death. Still, I'd chosen this path, chosen to live as I had been doing these last few years and that was what I needed to focus on now. Not the past. Not the future. But this exact moment because who the fuck knew whether or not the future would come, and being stuck in the past had absolutely nothing to do with me surviving in the here and now.

I could only do what I could do.

And today?

Well, today, what I could do was bend over, grab one of those plastic containers of food, and start eating.

"Apple pie," I whispered reverently as I opened the lid.

I'd just started to dip my finger into the warm, hot gooeyness of the filling—also, hey, no judgment, it wasn't like there were forks around—when the door flew open, and I found myself trapped in the steely eyes of Anabelle.

"What the fuck are you doing?"

More sharp. More glaring. More of me trying to bite back a smile.

More . . . cock-twitching.

I stifled the last two, glanced over her shoulder and saw the space behind her was empty. I could hear the voices farther inside the house, but for the moment we were alone, and this woman made me feel something.

Alive, you dumbass, my inner Brooke said. *She makes you feel alive.*

Yes, alive.

After I'd pretended to be dead—inside my soul as well as to the most important people in my life—for so fucking long. I didn't need an inner Brooke to keep me on the straight and narrow. Not any longer.

I had a real Brooke. A real Brent.

And real women who wouldn't stab me in the back the first chance it would serve them.

Although Anabelle—my eyes traced her face, noting the fury in her gaze, the clenched jaw, the lips pressed flat—I couldn't automatically discount that *this* woman might find the proper motivation to thrust a dagger right into my spine.

I felt a sliver of mischievousness slide through me at the thought.

Probably the wrong emotion, but I'd spent enough time with people who were wrong on the inside and out to not care that I felt humor at inappropriate moments.

Alive.

I'd made it through alive.

Albeit with a devil on my shoulder.

One that had me meeting Anabelle's deep brown eyes and smiling slow and hot. One that had me saying, "Oh, I'm sorry, Bella, did you want my fingers inside you instead?"

Her jaw fell open.

My smile widened.

Then she struck in a movement so fast and so unexpected that I didn't have a chance to block it, not when my reflexes had been tempered, coated in honey by need and desire, by her sexy body mere feet away, by her gorgeous flashing eyes.

I didn't react in time.

And I ended up with apple pie dumped all over the front of my pants.

THREE

Anabelle

"STICK YOUR FINGERS IN THAT," I muttered, grabbing the rest of the containers and going back inside the house. "Get your ass inside and talk to your sister," I called over my shoulder. "She's wrecked."

A beat of quiet then, "What's it to you?"

Slowly, I set the containers on the cute little table Iris kept in the hall, having to squeeze them in between the copious amount of Christmas decorations that she had already placed there then spun to face the man who I'd learned was Hayden, Brooke's supposedly dead brother. He was sinfully sexy with lush lips, a rugged jawline, piercing blue eyes, and all that brown hair laced with red. A fucking cover model.

I *should* be leaving.

I should go, to get out of here and let Brooke and Brent deal with Hayden. This man wasn't my brother, wasn't my friend.

He was . . . the one who'd hurt my family.

So, I was staying.

To protect my family. To keep watch over the people who'd

dragged me all but kicking and screaming into this little group. Who'd looked out for me, given me a job, baked me copious amounts of apple pie—my favorite, despite its current location on Hayden's crotch. Although . . . my eyes dropped, as though they had a mind of their own, and my mind . . . well, that hussy considered what it might be like to lick that filling off naked skin.

A snort. My gaze flying north to see the smirk on his face.

Which was appropriate. Because seriously? Me, a tiny Filipino girl with this behemoth of a gorgeous white dude. He looked like he should be in Hollywood, and I was just me. Short, curvy when I was feeling kind to myself, fat for the other ninety-nine percent of the time. Okay, I mentally sighed, I wasn't exactly fat. But I also wasn't the waifish beauty of Brooke or the perfect 36-24-36 of Iris.

I was—

Enough, my baby. You're always enough.

My mom's voice was the perfect bucket of ice-cold water . . . or reality in this case.

Because, seriously. What. In. The. Fuck. Was. Wrong. With. Me? Letting a man quantify my worth? Pathetic.

Sighing, I let my lips twist up into a smirk of my own. One I'd perfected in my years of bartending. One that perfectly encapsulated my disdain for the man still standing on the front porch, only now with apple pie filling dripping from his pants onto the concrete.

"If I liked what I saw," I told him, my lie carefully hidden by my icy tone, "believe me, I would have made that clear. As it is"—a shrug—"all I can say is that it's a . . . *little* cold, perhaps?"

Size. As in, making fun of it was so cliché.

And add another lie, aside from the whole not-liking-what-I-saw thing, to my repertoire. Because the wet cargo pants cupping his—

Cough.

Nope. Definitely not cold.

I spun, started walking down the hall again, knowing the *little* insult only worked if I managed to keep my gaze to myself.

Hot breath on my nape, husky words in my ear.

"Actually, I find that I'm quite warm."

I jumped, knocking into the table, bumping the containers, rattling the sheer volume of Christmas on the wooden surface. It matched the quantity of decorations she had in every corner of her house. Shining gold bobbles, red and silver glitter, multiple decorative trees from the one on the tiny tabletop—which I caught and steadied—to a huge pine tree taking up the entire corner of her living room.

But none of that changed the fact Hayden had moved and I hadn't sensed him.

That this gorgeous man was about six inches from my spine and every one of my nerves was on fire.

I wanted him.

Just like that.

Well, from the moment I'd laid eyes on him.

Which was wrong for a multitude of reasons, not the least of which was the pain he'd caused the two people in the other room. Two people who'd become integral to my life.

So, I needed to go back to thinking about little penises and annoying men and not about the fact that my lady bits were all but shouting, "Hey, girl, *hey!*"

Or not.

Maybe it was, "Hey, fuckable man, *hey—*"

Fingers drifting along my jaw. "What are you thinking?"

I jumped again, and this time I did knock over the tiny Christmas tree, clattering tiny gold balls in all directions.

"Fuck," I muttered, crouching to grab them.

Balls. Grabbing.

Cool.

I sensed him before I heard him this time. His soft "sorry" sliding over my skin like velvet. But I didn't get a chance to reply, to formulate the biting comeback I knew was necessary to create distance between this stranger and my suddenly awakened libido. Instead, I heard Brooke, her voice as jagged as Hayden's had been soft.

"Why?" she said. "Why—" A shake of her head. "How are you—"

A tear trailed down her cheek, and I didn't begrudge him one bit for immediately standing, for going over to his sister.

If anything, I begrudged him for waiting outside when I'd ordered him to, for delaying in the hall. He'd done so much already, caused so much pain, that the last thing he should have done was continue to stay away, just because I'd told him so.

He should have barreled through, held Brooke tight, and explained every fucking thing.

Or maybe that was *my* hang up.

Maybe that was what I'd wanted my dad and my brother to do. To show up. To own up. To treat me as an equal, or at least with kindness rather than a fury that made me feel beyond guilty. I wanted them to be the people I'd needed them to be. Except . . . maybe they were incapable. Maybe, it was simply an impossible ask.

Perhaps it was an impossible ask for Hayden as well.

I grabbed the last glass ball and shoved it along with the handful of others I'd retrieved back into the basket Iris had originally arranged them in, albeit with significantly less finesse. The next instant, I found my own feet, started to slide toward the door.

"Is that your doing?" Iris whispered, making me jump—and for fuck's sake, I was never this jumpy. I needed to get a grip . . .

or to at least get my gaze off the man standing a foot away from Brooke.

Shoring myself with a breath, I glanced over at Iris.

Up. No lies. I glanced *up*. Because even though she was short, I was shorter. Yay, genetics.

"Is what my doing?"

A delicately arched blond brow lifted. "The apple pie? The groin shot? Don't tell me that's not Anabelle Kim to a T."

"I don't know what you're talking about," I told her, taking another sly step toward the door. "I would never waste your apple pie."

"Filling," Iris muttered. "Just the filling since *somebody*"—read: Brent—"decided it was a good idea to ruin all of my hard work by turning off my freaking timer. Who does that?" She sighed. "And so not the point, I know. But Brent—I mean, Hayden. Well, *no* Brent. He just held on to so much guilt for so long and Hayden just shows up—" She bit her lip, and I found myself slipping an arm around her waist, hugging her gently, even though being touchy-feely had definitely not been in my vocabulary before meeting this crew.

But I was growing up.

Becoming an adult.

Learning feelings.

Or at least more feelings aside from fury, disappointment, and my ever-present favorite, sarcasm.

Because sarcasm wouldn't work in this moment.

"I'm sure there's an explanation," I said carefully. No, I wasn't sure, not in the least, but I also knew that comfort was needed in this moment more than anything else. Fury, disappointment, and sarcasm would come in spades later.

Iris narrowed her eyes. "It better be a damned good one."

I gave her one more squeeze before slipping into the kitchen and retrieving a towel. Not that the apple pie soaking into

Hayden's pants bothered *me* any, but I didn't want the sticky filling dripping onto Iris's rug. It was a bright, cheerful pattern of red, green, and gold, and I didn't think she'd appreciate picking apple chunks out of the fibers.

"Here," I said, shoving it into his hand and going to stand by Brooke. I crossed my arms and glared, knowing I was interrupting, but also not caring. Yes, Kace was on her other side, his arm around her waist, gaze equally as icy. But Brooke was hurting. She needed me.

My eyes flicked to Brent, saw that while my friend still looked a bit shell-shocked, he'd sidled close to Iris, and she'd wrapped her arms around his middle.

Satisfied he was taken care of, I returned my attention to Hayden, felt my temper fray. His eyes were on me, the blue darkened with heavy emotion, his face serious though I could have sworn I detected a note of amusement directed my way.

I sighed.

Everyone was just standing in the hallway, staring at each other, but no one was actually talking or *doing* anything.

"So, you're not dead," I said, feeling Brooke jump next to me.

Blue eyes, laughter visible in their depths stayed on mine. "No."

I made a hurry-up motion with my hands. "Okay, great. What gives? Why pretend that you were?"

Every trace of humor faded from his face, and I felt even my stone-cold heart twitch at the regret and pain that took its place. Hayden's gaze flicked to the floor then back up. This time it didn't come to me. It lasered to Brooke, holding for a long moment as he said, "It was the last thing I wanted to do, but believe me when I say that I had no other choice and that I came back as soon as I possibly could."

"From where?" Brent asked.

Hayden turned to look at him. "You know where."

An explosion of movement.

One second Brent was being held by Iris, and the next he was in Hayden's face, his hand around the other man's neck as he shoved Brooke's brother against the wall. Christmas-themed pictures rattled, Iris gasped, and Kace cursed.

"Tell me you didn't," Brent growled. "Tell me you didn't fucking do it."

"Do what?" Brooke asked when Hayden didn't answer, didn't move. "Hayden didn't do what, Brent?"

Furious brown eyes flicked from Hayden to Brooke. "Work for those people."

Brooke opened her mouth, probably to ask exactly the question I was thinking—which was, *What people?*—but she didn't get a chance to form words.

"I had to, B," Hayden said. "They needed me. We came home. I worked for them here for a bit—small, local stuff. Then something bigger came up and they arranged for me to disappear."

"That's why you went off active duty?" Brent asked. "You said you were struggling with—" He cut himself off.

Hayden was quiet for a few seconds. "I was," he said. "They helped. The stuff I was doing helped."

Brooke spoke up then. "So that whole time you were back. The whole time you pushed me away after the explosion." A sharp shake of her head. "You're my twin and you would barely let me see you, but you were fine and working for who exactly?"

"I can't tell you that," Hayden said.

Brent dropped his hand, stepped back. "Fuck, man. You're a fucking idiot. You should have come to me."

"I couldn't." Hayden shrugged. "Keeping the secret made it easier on everyone because it was unlikely that I was coming home anyway."

"Easier for who?" Brent asked. "It's been ten years since you *died*."

That wasn't the question I thought most pertinent in this scenario, not when I wanted to know why Hayden had thought it was unlikely he would make it home alive from wherever he'd been the last years. Still, I didn't say that or ask my own query. Instead, I watched, almost riveted at the flurry of emotions that passed through his expression.

Regret. Guilt. Pain. Misery. Loss. Searching.

Hope.

All gone in a flash. All locked down behind a blank mask.

Except for hope. I could still see a sliver of it creeping into those baby blues. He might have teased me, might have affected a light, almost carefree appearance on the porch, but this man wasn't what he portrayed. He might be good at burying those feelings, at hiding them in an instant, but that didn't mean they weren't there.

I could sense the hurricane of sentiments spiraling just beneath the surface.

"Easier for me," he said quietly. "I knew I wouldn't be able to do what they needed me to do unless Brooke was taken care of."

Brooke's voice was fierce, only the barest wobble at the end. "And by taken care of, you mean heartbroken?"

"Brookie—" Hayden began.

"Don't, Hay." Brooke shook her head. "I can't do this right now. I thought I'd failed you, that I wasn't there for you a-and I blamed—" She sniffed, shoulders lifting and falling on a long inhale and exhale. "I-I don't know what to think. Are you back for good?" she asked. "Or are you going to disappear and make me think you're dead again?"

"I'm out," he said, "and I'm not going back."

Iris crossed over to him, rested her hand on the small of

Brent's back. He sighed. "Why did you do it, Hay? I told you they were bad news."

"Who's they?" I said, finally bursting back into the conversation.

A heavy gaze to mine.

"And," I went on, "why the fuck did you think you were going to end up dead doing whatever it was that you were doing with them?"

Silence, then, "I don't think I owe you any explanations."

I didn't back down. My mom had given me lots of spine, and I wasn't afraid to use that spine for good. Not when this man had hurt my family. "Maybe not," I said. "But you owe them"—I nodded at Brooke and Brent—"and I think you'd better stop dancing around the issue and level with them."

He moved. Like Brent had moved.

I blinked, and in one moment he was in front of me, staring down, eyes cold and full of fury. "I don't know you, little girl," he said, each word carefully enunciated and filled with frost. "You have no right to give me orders."

"First, I'm a woman," I gritted. "Second, I may be little, but I'm not afraid of you."

A flash of darkness on his face. "You should be."

"Enough, Hayden," Brooke murmured. "Just . . . enough. It's late. We all have questions, but you're here now." A long, slow sigh. "We can talk in the morning."

Hayden nodded.

"Will you come stay at my and Kace's place?" she asked.

"My car is already there," he said.

I narrowed my eyes because more questions. How did he know where Brooke lived? And for that matter, how did he know to find Brooke here?

My friend didn't seem particularly bothered. She just nodded, said, "Ours is, too." And then she slipped her arms around Hayden and hugged him. He turned his hips, avoided plastering her with apple pie filling, and I had to give him props for that small gesture.

Considerate.

Except when faking his own death.

Cool.

They broke apart, and Kace reached out, taking Brooke's hand, tugging her back against him. Normally, I would have rolled my eyes at the gesture. Tonight, I was glad that he was there and would have her back.

Hayden turned to Brent, and I allowed my gaze to follow, to see that Iris had moved into a similar position, holding his hand, except she'd also tucked herself into Brent's side, had taken her free arm and wrapped it tightly around her newfound—as in only a few hours old—fiancé.

Brooke was covered.

Brent was covered.

I should slip out now.

And because I was just as good at protecting as I was at leaving before the people around me realized I'd overstayed my welcome, I quietly moved to the hall table, letting the soft murmur of Brooke's voice, her assertion that they would most definitely be talking in the morning and that Hayden had better be prepared to explain everything trailing my movements.

I picked up my leftovers—because I wasn't about to let any more of them go to waste—then made my way to the front door.

This time, I set the containers down on the porch to shut the door behind me.

Then I bent, snagged them, and was in my car less than thirty seconds later.

A silent drive home. A silent walk through the yard to the guesthouse I'd rented, located behind my landlord's house.

So much silence.

But then again, aside from my makeshift family, silence had pretty much been my whole life for the last few years.

My mom gone. My dad living with my sister on the East Coast. My brother busy with his career as an honest-to-God rocket scientist.

And me.

Bartender extraordinaire. College drop-out. Youngest and least successful of the Kim trio. I *should* be pursuing my PhD at Stanford, should be climbing that corporate ladder and giving the CEO a high five as I overtook him in the boardroom *and* then snagged his job.

But . . . college had seemed much less important after I'd lost my mom.

Eighteen. Accepted to Stanford. Both parents so damned proud of me.

And then within a few weeks, one of my best friends had been gone from the planet. Ovarian cancer. Metastasized to the liver, the kidneys, the lymph nodes. Stage Four. Nothing the doctors could do about it.

My mom had died, and the only positive was that it had been quick.

Not painless.

But thankfully, not long either.

We'd buried her. We'd done the wake, the funeral, the mass, the celebration of life on a rugged California beach that had been her favorite. We'd done right by her.

Except, we hadn't been able to save her, to protect her from the disease that was slowly killing her from the inside out. And though I'd tried to go to college, though I'd managed to make it through one year, knowing that my mom had been beyond excited for me to go to Stanford. Exclusive, top-notch, worked my ass to get into.

But . . . I just couldn't do it.

How could I prioritize statistics class when my mom wasn't here? How could I focus on calculus or microbiology when neither of those two things had saved my mom?

I wasn't noble. I didn't want to devote my life to research, to go on a life-long quest to cure cancer.

I just wanted my mom back.

And since that wasn't going to happen . . . I'd disappeared for a while.

Like Hayden, my mental voice that sounded like my mother said. The memories were bad. The physical punch of actually hearing her—manifestation of my brain or not—was a thousand times worse.

"Fuck," I muttered, stowing the leftovers in the fridge and heading for my bedroom.

Not liking the truth, but knowing it was truth anyway.

Yes, I had been like Hayden.

Disappearing, though I had kept in contact with my family, hadn't given them cause to worry.

Not true, Ana Girl.

Yes, to that as well. I'd given them plenty to worry about, had permanently broken the ties between us when I'd left for a year. Even now, I couldn't go visit and not see the pain I'd caused. The dreams I'd crushed. I knew they loved me, just as I loved them. But I couldn't find that closeness again, couldn't reconcile their inability to respect my need to search for and find myself with the pressure they'd put on me to keep my head down and keep moving forward after Mom had died.

It was just as well that my brother and sister were living in New York.

A country separating them from their disappointing sister.

"Enough," I said, quickly stripping and pulling on pajamas, setting my alarm for what would now be a godawful early time in the morning.

But while I might not be putting my head down walking through the corridors of Stanford or a fancy lab or a Fortune 500 company, I was making a living. I had a place to live, a job. I had friends who knew me better than my own flesh and blood, who'd become my second family.

Maybe I hadn't found that missing piece yet, but I'd found a slice of happy.

And as far as I was concerned, that was good enough.

My cell buzzed and I looked down to see a text message from my sister. It was a picture of a big dining room table with all of the foods from my childhood Christmases, each perfectly laid out on a platter, gorgeous cutlery surrounding pristine plates, and elegant flower arrangements. Each of the napkins was even intricately folded.

Perfect. Precise. Exceeded expectations.

And . . . me.

"Fuck," I muttered, knowing that for all my talk of a second family, I still missed my biological one . . . or at least, what we'd once been to each other.

My phone buzzed again.

You should have been here.

Maybe, I should have been. My dad wasn't getting any younger, and who knew how many holidays he had left.

But . . . our relationship was strained, as it had been for years. I'd known when I decided to go to Iris's tonight that I couldn't look into his eyes, into my brother's, even into my sister's—who was pushy and a perfectionist, but who was really driven by a need to care for everyone around her—and cope with seeing the disappointment. Not this year. I loved my family, even as I accepted they couldn't be what I needed, but I couldn't go through that again.

I needed Brooke and Kace, Iris and Brent. I needed a judgment-free zone and teasing and paper napkins with Christmas penguins tossed haphazardly onto a table we served ourselves from.

I needed laughter and friends.

I needed a burned cherry pie and a hidden engagement ring.

So, I'd stayed, and now I typed out a generic response.

I'll visit soon. Merry Christmas, Kelly.

Good. You need a haircut. I'll take you to my lady and she'll fix you up.

Sighing, I plugged in my phone, lay back on my bed, and forced myself to go to sleep.

I was happy. I was content.

That was enough.

FOUR

Hayden

I HEARD the creak of the floorboard, the soft exclamation of "crap," but I didn't startle.

I was already awake, camped out on Brooke's couch.

Time zones were the reason for my insomnia. My sister's sleeplessness was a regular and common occurrence. She'd always been a night owl, but more so after she'd become a published author and had moved in with a bartender who worked until last call.

How did I know this?

I'd tapped her phone.

It was the same way I knew that her ex, a fucking scumbag of a human being, had been denied parole at his last hearing two months ago. And how I'd known that she'd moved to the Bay Area, that she'd hit bestseller lists, that she'd recently reunited with Brent.

She would be furious when she found out.

As would Brent.

I hadn't been able to do anything but watch and I'd needed to make keeping those tabs enough.

But . . . it hadn't been nearly enough.

I knew that as much as I knew anything in my bones, and as much as I'd known that I hadn't wanted to leave them . . . well, I'd thought that it had been my only choice. They'd needed me at KTS. I was the best fit for the job, and the sacrifice on my end was for the greater good.

Of course, that had been ego talking.

Because there were plenty of people with my skills.

And KTS hadn't been the utopian organization, always fighting for that greater good that I'd hoped it would be.

Reality.

Fuck, it stung sometimes.

Luckily, a few of the lifers at KTS had smoothed my exit, after having discovered that the way I'd been recruited didn't exactly align with their principles, especially as they were trying to clean up the group, to truly fight for those innocents who needed them.

Apparently, even the good guys had a few bad apples scattered within.

The paramilitary organization was currently undergoing some major housecleaning, rooting out those bad apples, and when I'd heard about my commander, Daniel's, being at the center of it all, I'd been able to reach out to the right people to ensure I got my walking papers. And to ensure I wouldn't be drawn back in.

I was *done* done.

It wasn't that I didn't want to help people. I did, wouldn't have gotten into the military if I hadn't. I just . . . wanted it to be on my own terms.

Not exactly following the chain of command, now was I?

But fuck, I at least preferred to not be coerced into putting my life on the line. Of course, I'd prefer to go into it eyes wide open, the decision of my own making, rather than being manipulated. I'd also certainly prefer that the man who'd convinced me to join in the first place had not been a total fucking scumbug.

A *thunk*.

Another muffled curse. Then rapid-fire clicking.

I sat up.

Brooke's face was illuminated by the computer screen, her fingers flying over the keyboard. "Just need to get this down," she whispered to herself, and I could see the tip of her tongue poking out the corner of her mouth.

Fucking hell, my sister had been adorable when we were growing up—my partner in crime, mischievous and sweet, her long red hair usually pulled up into pigtails—and she was beyond adorable now with her hair askew, mismatched pajamas on, and that same look of concentration on her face that I'd seen from the moment she'd first tried to make us peanut butter and jelly sandwiches.

My little—by only ten minutes as she liked to remind me— sister. But still my baby sister, still someone I was supposed to protect, especially after our parents died.

My heart clenched. Hard. Painfully. Because . . . fuck, I'd hurt her.

The worst part was I could never make up for that.

After a final few clicks, Brooke spun, a gasp escaping when she saw me sitting up on the couch. "Hayden," she said, hand coming up to her chest. "Oh, I'm sorry. Did I wake you?"

I pushed up from the cushions, crossed over to her. "No, I couldn't sleep."

Green eyes that looked almost emerald when illuminated by the dim light of the computer screen softened, and she took my hand. "Come on."

She led me into the kitchen, flicking on a set of under cabinet lights as we went, filling the space with a dim golden glow. I didn't protest that she should go back to sleep, that she should leave me to my dark thoughts and get back to the man who clearly adored her—even if I hadn't seen that within ten seconds of interacting with Kace, I'd witnessed it many times over the last year.

Photos from the man I had on Brooke's protection detail showing how Kace looked at her. That being, right and with utter adoration in his eyes. Texts I'd read putting that adoration into words to be read. Tapes of calls that I'd needed to cut off because I was both mentally scarred and wanted to kill the man for having had sex, much less for having discussed anything to do with sex with my sister. She was happy. They loved each other.

So, I knew I should let her go back to bed.

But I couldn't.

I'd missed her.

"Sit," she ordered, nudging me toward a barstool before reaching into a cabinet she could only reach on her tippy toes.

"Brookie—" I began.

A stern gaze tossed over one shoulder. *"Sit."*

Sighing, I quietly tugged out the stool and sat down on it. I'd never been able to deny her anything.

Says the man who pretended to be dead for a decade.

My shoulders stiffened at the thought, said in the quiet rasp of the woman I'd met that evening. I'd seen her in a few pictures, but I'd discounted her importance, hadn't expected to see her tonight.

Brown skin with undertones of gold, small and curvy, lips that appeared as soft as pillows—and if they were pillows, I definitely wanted to rest certain body parts there.

No surprise, it wasn't my head.

Or at least not that one.

"Fucking hell," I muttered, pitching the curse low enough to not be overheard. I was in the room with my sister. My single living family member, who I'd hurt, possibly beyond all hope of reconciliation.

And I was thinking of fucking.

With my sister humming six feet away, clad in penguin pajama bottoms and a gnome-patterned baseball tee.

Cool.

I deliberately pushed thoughts of Anabelle away, knowing that while my attraction to her was two-fold (she was beautiful and she had fire—both were my kryptonite), it wasn't something I was in a position to explore. Not when I was trying to figure out how to put my life back together, and certainly not when she was close to my sister. I'd done enough. The last thing I needed to do was seduce my sister's friend.

Inner chastising complete, I focused on what Brooke was doing and felt my heart clench, my stomach twist itself into knots.

Hot chocolate.

She glanced up from where she'd pulled two mugs of milk out of the microwave. "I'm okay, Hay," she whispered. "It was . . . a shock to say the least, but"—a sniff—"I'm not m-mad. R-really. I'm so glad you're okay, so glad I get another chance to tell you how much I love you."

I pushed to my feet and hurried over to her, pulling her against my chest and hugging her tight. "I'm so sorry I hurt you, Brookie," I whispered against the soft red silk of her hair. "I didn't want to. I swear."

"I know."

Her fingers clenched onto my T-shirt. "I love you, big bro."

Another spasm in my heart. After the last decade I would

have sworn the organ had dried up, had withered to so much dust. But I'd simply forgotten the power of Brooke.

"I love you, too."

She sniffed, slipped out of my hold, and turned back to the mugs. One hand reached out to open a unicorn-shaped cookie jar on the counter, and I grinned when I saw her extract two paper and foil packets.

"Powdered hot cocoa mix? How beneath you," I teased, tugging a strand of her hair.

She tossed a grin in my direction. "I know it's very third grade, but it's how you always used to make it when Mom and Dad were sleeping, and it was just the two of us." A shrug. "I never grew out of it, even after I was on my own."

I hadn't known that.

Even though I'd been in her life after we were grown, I'd also been deployed more than I'd been home. I'd missed this quirk that touched my not-withered heart.

Her cheeks flushed and she dropped her head, concentrating on opening the packages and pouring one into each mug of milk. It was as she was stirring the powder into the liquid that I managed to find my voice. "I thought for sure you'd have outgrown it."

Another shrug. "I know there are better and fancier ways to make hot chocolate, but they never taste right."

Fuck, my eyes actually burned, but I forced my tone to be light as I slung an arm—albeit carefully—around my sister's shoulders. "It's the preservatives," I told her, pressing a kiss to the top of her head before I swooped down and stole a mug.

"Wait!" She batted my chest, snagged the mug back. "You're missing my secret ingredient."

"I don't recall a secret ingredient when I used to make this for you."

A grin. "That's because you're not as brilliant as me."

"Well," I said, "we've both always known that." I snatched the mug and took a sip, one that was punctuated by her annoyed sigh before I set it back down on the counter. "Ah. The taste of powder on my tongue. Oh, how I've missed you."

She smacked me again. "Shut it, you. Now, go." A shove back toward the barstool. "I don't share my secret ingredient with just anyone."

I tickled her, just beneath her ribs and she squealed before clamping a hand over her mouth. "Stop!" she said, the plea muffled as she danced away from me. Dropping her hands, she glared, though her eyes were twinkling with amusement. "You're lucky Kace is a heavy sleeper," she scolded.

Not heavy enough, I thought, noticing him on the edges of my periphery. He was sleep-rumpled and shirtless, and when I turned my head to meet his gaze, he held my stare for several long moments. "About that . . ." I began.

But then Brooke giggled. His face softened, the rest of my words were lost, and I focused on my sister. She could fucking light up the room.

I glanced back when I saw the shadows shift. Kace stayed just long enough to nod.

Then he was gone, and I was forced to begrudgingly think the man was a good one to give me and my sister the space to talk, to not interfere or interject. Of course, his expression had also said he'd gut me six ways to Sunday if I hurt Brooke again, but I couldn't resent that.

I *had* hurt her.

She needed protecting.

And God, how much would she love to hear me thinking that.

Grinning, I headed for the stool. "What's the secret ingredient?"

"Not gonna happen, Hay," she said, going back to the mugs

and deliberately blocking my vision from what she was doing. I heard a drawer open, some plastic rustling, but before I could get too curious, she was heading toward me.

The mug plunked down in front of me.

She plunked down *next* to me.

And I felt my lips tug up further when I saw what was inside, Brooke's so-called secret ingredient.

A giant marshmallow.

"Now, I know what you're thinking," she said. "But it's mint flavored and amazing and makes this taste like the really expensive peppermint hot chocolate you can only get this time of year."

I didn't give two shits about expensive hot chocolate or mint or the fact that there was special Christmas hot chocolate.

I only cared that I was here.

With Brooke.

And somehow, she didn't hate me.

Still, she was looking at me so expectantly that I picked up the mug, took a huge sip, prepared to hide my wince because mint was so not my favorite.

To my surprise, it was fucking delicious.

I slurped back more, looked up to see Brooke had her hands wrapped around her mug, a pleased expression on her face. "Good, right?" she asked between sips.

I nodded. "The best."

I didn't mean the hot chocolate. She knew that. I could see it in her eyes, her expression, her gentle voice when she asked, "You can't really tell me about it, can you?"

"I want to," I said, guilt slicing my insides. I owed her an explanation, I knew I did. Except, there wasn't much I could tell her that would be safe.

I had signed the NDA of all NDAs in order to get out and—

Fingers on my arm. "It's okay."

"Brookie—" I shook my head and pushed my mug away, the hot chocolate now sitting like a brick in my stomach. "It's not. I know that," I said. "I—I guess this is like the start of a Hollywood action flick. Only I'm done with the action part. I just want to be home, to start fresh and build a life with you."

Her eyes dropped.

"What?" I asked.

Silence. Long enough that I was itching to push her into answering, itching to demand. Before everything had happened, I wouldn't have hesitated. Now? There was a lot of un-hashed history.

So, I stayed silent.

And she answered me anyway.

"I'm just wondering how long it will be that you'll stick around building this life," she said quietly. "I'm not trying to be a jerk, but you've never had staying power. You were always flitting off on some adventure or another."

That drive for adventure, for the next challenge that would send my adrenaline soaring was part of why I'd gotten mixed up with KTS in the first place.

But I was done with adrenaline.

I was done with adventures.

I was done doing things just to solely feed my ego.

I wanted normal and safe and family and familiar. I wanted to hang out with my sister and drive her crazy. I wanted to make sure this Kace treated her right and threaten to cut off his balls if he made the tiniest frown appear on her face.

"I mean it, Brookie," I told her. "I'm out for good."

"Yeah." A pause that was long enough to tell me she didn't believe me. Then, she played her fingers over the handle of her mug and asked, "Did you at least get the bad guys?"

My gut clenched.

The answer to that was complicated.

I'd gotten *some* of the bad guys. The problem was that so many others were running free. I might as well have stuck my finger in the proverbial dam for all the good I'd done over the last decade. Take out one disgusting human trafficker, and five more popped up. Bust one drug ring that was destroying the local economy, hurting innocents, poisoning people, and another quickly took its place. Destroy thousands of servers with child pornography, and other pictures appeared almost instantly on the Dark Web.

It was doing good . . .

And it was doing nothing at all.

Brooke looked up at me with a soft expression, her fingers drifting to my arm again. "It's not your job to save the world."

Except that was exactly what I'd signed up for.

FIVE

Anabelle

I GLANCED down at my cell, saw that it was almost last call, and sighed in relief.

Two days since Christmas, the first night Bobby's was open, and people must have felt the need to cut loose after so much family time.

The place had been slammed from the moment I'd started my shift, and it had stayed slammed. Standing room only at the bar, all the tables full. Hell, I'd poured so many drinks that I'd had to send Kace into the storeroom to get more liquor. And through it all, Brooke stayed ruthlessly focused on her laptop, slurping down one Diet Coke after the next, until thirty minutes ago when she'd smiled dazedly up at Kace, who'd brought her one of those sodas laced with rum.

Rum and notes.

Heh.

Smirking to myself, I finished pouring the last of my orders then began to close out my station. Stacking the dirty glasses in the plastic racks, shoving those one by one into the dishwasher that had been installed under the counter. It ran on a quick cycle, and it didn't take long to catch up on the dirties. Of course, there would be plenty more to do once this crowd finished up their final drinks.

Thus was the torture of a bartender.

On my feet. Lots of dishes. Having to shut up and take orders in order to make a living.

Oh, if my mom could see me now.

She used to try to get me to help in the kitchen, to stand next to her and learn all the recipes that had been passed down from her grandmother to her mother to her and finally to my sister.

But that was where the line of succession had ended.

I'd not seen the value in learning to cook, in memorizing those recipes. I hadn't cared to know how much water to add to rice or what it had to do with knuckles. I certainly hadn't wanted to waste time in the kitchen when I'd had so many more important things to do.

Essays to write. Tests to ace. Extracurriculars to lock down.

Plus, if I made enough money, I could just order takeout, right?

Oh, how naïve I'd been at eighteen. Thinking I knew everything. Convinced each and every decision I made was the right one.

What I wouldn't give to have some of that confidence again.

"Nothing you can do to change the fucking past," I muttered, shoving in a tray and jabbing at the start button on the dishwasher.

"No, you can't."

The only reason I didn't jump was because I'd felt him. Felt *Hayden*.

Shoring myself against the impact of him, I looked up.

Shoring didn't make one fucking lick of difference.

I was surprised my eyes didn't sizzle out of my head, burned to ash by the pure pretty standing across from me. Then the fucker had to add in a sexy smile, a slice of badass, and . . . kryp-to-nite.

As in, he was exactly the type of man who was mine.

"Your sister's over there," I said, jerking my head to Brooke's corner, to the barstool that was saved for her in perpetuity.

"And if I said I wasn't here to see Brooke?"

Long, slow, and hot, and I could easily imagine that same *long, slow, and hot* in other places aside from my eardrums.

Like a *long, slow, and hot* tongue dragging over my cl—

Good fucking grief.

I blinked, forced myself to rewind the conversation back to what he'd said. *Ah.* Not there to see Brooke.

"Yeah, right," I muttered, turning my back on him and beginning to print out tickets for the open tabs, shoving them into black pleather holders that I then stacked at my side to deliver.

When I'd finished, I turned back and nearly dropped the lot.

He was still there.

My pussy liked that, liked looking at him, liked thinking about what all that lean strength might be like in bed.

His mouth curved, revealed a dimple at the corner.

Fuck. He'd be good.

I could feel that in my bones.

"Brooke's busy," he said, and his voice was pure fucking sex. Which should have been gross, since he was discussing his sister, but instead it came across as private, as tempting, a goddamned siren's call.

I flicked a glance to the side, saw Brooke's laptop had been stowed, that she was sucking down that rum and Diet Coke. "No, she's done for the night."

"How do you know?" he asked.

"How *don't* you know?" I countered.

A flash of guilt across his face, and dammit, now *I* was feeling guilty. But, I didn't have anything to feel guilty about. I hadn't left Brooke, hadn't hurt Brooke—

You just hurt your own family.

And wasn't that a wonderful feeling for two in the morning?

I turned away again, though this time it was due to remorse and not rabid sexual longing—though I could honestly say I didn't know which was worse. Either way, I made quick work of delivering the bills, and then made sure to avoid returning to the spot where Hayden was standing.

Oh, look at that! I desperately needed to restock the wine.

Oh and the rum *and* the vodka. Oh and we were low on O.J. and—

I slipped out from behind the bar, grabbed my tub that I used to carry as many of the heavy bottles as I could manage in one trip—and yes, every time I went grocery shopping, I did battle to make sure it was that single voyage from my car through the backyard to my cottage.

My biceps were rockin'.

My legs were still short.

Snorting to myself, I headed down the hall, used the keypad on the doorknob to input the code and unlock the storeroom, and slipped inside.

Wine first.

A surprisingly good variety for a bar, but then again, that wasn't difficult to do when we were just minutes from any number of great wineries. Since we sold more of it than someone might expect, considering we *were* a bar, I settled three bottles into the bottom of the bucket. Next came vodka. Mid-label because we still had plenty of the cheap college shit and two full bottles of top-shelf left. After that, I put in a few bottles of rum and one of O.J.

There was probably more we were low on, but my bucket was nearly full, and I knew my strength would already be tested as it was.

I lifted with a grunt—and also my legs. It was a heavy load, enough to make my arms strain almost immediately. But I didn't give in, didn't put it down. First, because I was a stubborn asshole. Second, because I had to make it back to the bar. *With* the booze. I had enough nightmares in my life. I didn't need to add me throwing my back out and ending up prone on the store-room floor until someone came and rescued me—and the bottles —to my dark dreams.

With another grunt, I pushed through the door, making sure it latched behind me.

"Let me get that—"

This time I did jump when Hayden spoke from behind me.

I'd been too focused on the burn of my arms to realize that the burn had also drifted south . . . and in between.

The bottles clinked, and I struggled to not drop everything, especially when Hayden came close, started to try and pull it from my grip.

"I got it," I snapped.

"I can help—" He grunted when I elbowed him hard in the stomach.

"Back up, asshole." I shoved by him. Or tried to anyway.

He didn't let go of the bucket, and for all my shoving *by* him, I ended up pressed against him, the tub at my side, my arms pinned between us.

"I'm trying to help you."

"I don't need your help," I growled, yanking hard and not getting anywhere except closer to this man in a narrow hallway.

One that was feeling infinitely narrower with him so near. "Not now. Not *ever*."

"What? Is it tough to be gracious?"

My mouth dropped open, and I nearly lost my grip on the bucket, but then I pulled my head out of my ass, lifted my chin, and used every bit of spare strength to tear it from Hayden's hands.

Then nearly dropped it.

But I had more than a little grit left. I steeled myself, refused to let it fall.

Because *gracious?* Seriously?

"Go fuck yourself, Hayden." I began walking—okay, began *duck*-walking my way back into the bar.

"God save us from stubborn women," he muttered, all of six inches from my ear.

And my temper—what little was left of it, anyway —snapped.

I plunked the bucket onto the floor, turned around to give this pretty, sexy, arrogant, annoying-as-shit man a piece of my mind. I'd dumped drinks on asshole customers for less. I wasn't going to take any shit from a man who'd faked his own death and devastated his sister and best friend.

"I—"

He bent, hefted the hamper of bottles like it weighed all of a pound, and strode down the hall, his long legs eating up the distance. And before I'd processed exactly what he'd done, he slipped back into the bar.

With my booze.

"Bastard," I hissed, stomping after him.

By the time I made it into the space, most of the customers had finished their drinks and were heading out. For the first time that night, more stools were empty than filled, and I saw that Iris had shown up, was cuddled next to Brent and looking decidedly sleepy.

I wanted to find out why she was there when her daytime job had her up at the crack of dawn on a regular basis and at last call on only the rare occurrence, but I was too pissed.

Because of *him*.

Who was currently casually unloading bottles at my station, stacking them in a careful line as though we hadn't just been playing tug of war out in the hallway.

I stormed over, used my shoulder to shove him out of the way.

Yes, I was fully aware that the man who'd been able to lift the bottles with such ease was probably letting me move him to the side.

I didn't care.

He was in my space, my spot, and frankly, his gall was pissing me off.

"Which is your favorite?" he asked, tone light and again revealing nothing of our hallway antics.

I ignored him.

A soft chuckle that slid down my spine, that lifted goose bumps on my nape, that had my thighs clenching together.

"I'll figure it out," he said. "I'm really good at guessing people's drinks."

I snorted, continued pulling out bottles.

"Not beer," he said, and I glanced out of the corner of my eye to see he was staring off at the shelves behind the bar, pointer finger tapping against his lips. "No, you don't mind beer, will drink it with friends. But that's not your favorite."

Blue eyes cut to the side, to mine, drawing my gaze to his, and I felt the air in my lungs freeze before I quickly returned my focus to the counter in front of me.

"Hmm," he said, still leaning next to me, arms and ankles

crossed, the bulge of his biceps emphasized by the way his black T-shirt bisected the muscles. I had the distinct urge to place my mouth there, to trace the veins and hard lines with my tongue.

My gaze slid in, over flat abs and a narrow waist, down to powerful thighs encased in another pair of cargo pants.

A cough. "My eyes are up here."

I rolled mine, picked up the orange juice and bent to shove it into the fridge installed beneath the counter.

"So, not beer," he said. "Wine is a possibility." He was fishing, but even knowing that, I still couldn't hold back my snort. "Not wine then. Rum?"

Since I currently had bottles of rum and wine in my hands, I said, "Is you being *really good* at guessing people's drinks actually just you naming every type of alcohol that exists until you stumble onto the right answer?"

A shrug. "If I have to."

I tsked. "Where's the skill in that? It's like watching a bad psychic try to fool someone by picking up on insignificant details. Next time, you'll tell me that someone who has the letter D in their name is speaking to me from the other side."

Silence. Long enough that I glanced up and saw he was smirking. "Ah, but now you've told me you do have a favorite drink. That's progress."

Silk. The smug words should have pissed me off.

Instead, they drifted down my skin like the soft fabric, and I barely held back my shiver.

Ugh.

Turning my back on him, I stashed the rum and wine onto the lower shelves behind me. Unfortunately, the mirrors behind the bottles showed me that Hayden had moved, was holding out two more bottles of wine for me to stow away. I met his gaze in the mirror and knew I was staring. I *should* have been glaring, but the blue of his eyes was striking—the ocean on a warm

Northern Californian day. Deep turquoise and navy swirled together. And then add in his crisp jawline, kissable lips, and hair that was thick enough to make my fingers itch to touch . . .

Irresistible.

"Here," he whispered, coming closer, near enough that I could feel the heat of his body through the layers of my clothing.

The bottle drifted forward, its label coming right in front of my face.

I blinked, snatched it from him.

"So, not beer, not wine, not rum. Hmm." The hot breath of that exhalation hit my skin and this time, I couldn't hold back my shiver. "I know," he murmured. "It's a Cosmopolitan."

I laughed outright.

A girl drink.

Me?

The man had lost his bloody mind. I mean, Cosmos were tasty, and kudos to those peeps who wanted to drink them, but I wasn't girly. I wasn't soft and froufrou.

I was a whiskey on the rocks.

That burn in the back of the throat, the heated trail dipping down into my stomach. I flamed hot and brief, and then when I was gone, consumed to the last drop, I went back to my regularly scheduled program of ice.

"Fuck, you have a sexy laugh." Low, hot words whispered right into my ear, his lips brushing my skin, sending trails of heat to my pussy as effectively as that whiskey.

My mouth dropped open, words failing me.

But that was just as well because Hayden had plenty of words.

"I haven't felt one goddamned thing in ten years aside from guilt and a need to make what I'd done worth it," he said and for all that it was quiet, his words were no less intense. "It wasn't."

"I—"

He kept talking, which was still just as well, because I might have gotten the one syllable out, but I certainly wasn't able to form full sentences at that point. "Then I saw you on that porch, looking like some contortionist out of Cirque de Soleil. And I stood there watching, knowing I should help you, but unable to for the longest time."

His head dropped, and he inhaled.

"You're insane," I blurted.

He laughed and my eyes flew up to meet his in the mirror. "Maybe." A beat. "But you're still the sexiest woman I've seen in my life."

That more than anything knocked me back into the present.

This might seem like an intimate moment between two people, especially given the way his big body blocked out everything around me. But we were still in a public place, still where I worked, still all of thirty feet away from his *sister* for God's sake.

All of that.

But his words were what kicked my brain back into gear.

Because they were laughable. I was not anyone's fantasy, let alone the sexiest woman he'd ever seen.

I was shaped like a cardboard box. Wide shoulders, wide hips, barely any curves in between. Men wanted women like the Kardashians or Giselle. They didn't want an average-shaped female with an average face and above-average hair.

Whatever I might think of my looks, my body, I at least knew my hair was on point. A rich ebony that seemed to absorb the light rather than reflect it, my thick locks gave no indication they were anything but healthy. Then when the sun or overhead lights hit them just right, they shone like a gleaming river rock on a bright summer day. I wore it long, knew it was part of the reason I got better tips because when I pulled it back and customers weren't distracted by my mane, when my "sparkling" personality was the only thing shining, I went home with far fewer Washingtons and Lincolns in my apron pocket.

My hair had been up at Iris's.

So, I hadn't even had that going for me.

"You're clearly delusional," I said, spinning around and stepping to the side so I could create some space between us. "Or spitting nonsense." I picked up the bottle of vodka and shoved it into his chest. "Find another girl if you need to get laid. I'm not interested."

Lies.

But lies in self-preservation.

"Anabelle—"

Heat running over me in scorching waves, burning me from the inside out. And that was just from the husky way he said my name.

Unbidden, I turned.

However, I didn't allow myself to be ensnared by that deep blue gaze. Instead, I forced the cold to the forefront and said, "Vodka goes on the top shelf."

And then I walked away.

And then because I was a fucking coward with a pussy that was very much in disagreement with my walking away from a man who'd said I was the sexiest woman he'd ever seen, not to mention that it had emerged from the lips of a man who looked like Hayden, I hightailed it straight over to Brooke and Kace.

They, luckily for me, were way too in love and thus, way too wrapped up in each other, to recognize the posturing happening behind the bar.

I used them as a barrier.

No shame. No deception in my brain.

No deception in Hayden's eyes either.

He watched me walk toward them—a fact I knew because

not only could I feel his gaze on me, but every time I glanced to the side, I could see him watching me in the mirror.

Six feet away those blue eyes caught mine.

And he smiled. Hot and slow and with purpose.

My insides perked up excitedly, all with the exception of my gut. That twisted itself into knots at the same pace as the alarm bells blaring in my mind.

That smile belonged to a predator.

And I had the distinct thought that I had somehow just become the prey.

SIX

Hayden

"IT'S A BLOODY MARY," I told her.

The bar was empty save me, Kace, Brooke, and Anabelle.

But I had a reason to be hanging around. Kace and Brooke were my ride.

Also, lucky for me, it gave me some additional time to get under the skin of a beautiful woman named Anabelle.

Her shoulders rose and fell on an exhale then she glanced up from the glass she was drying with a towel to meet my eyes. "What nonsense are you spouting now, McAlister?"

Ha. She might be trying to put me off me, but she would fail.

I'd always been good at pestering my sister into submission (in this case, into talking to me again) if she tried to give me the silent treatment, and now I was going to continue using that superpower . . . well, I *wanted* to say continue using it for good, but in reality, I was using it for mischief.

Or maybe it was for another reason.

One I didn't want to look at too closely.

One that made the space between my shoulder blades itch with the need to get off the stool, to retreat, to leave the bar and never come back.

But then I would lose my chance to make things up to Brooke.

Then I would also lose this chance at exploring why the fierce, tough Anabelle had a chip on her shoulder the size of an elephant, why she stared at me in distrust, why she felt the need to be so strong, so . . . separate from the rest of the world.

"Your favorite drink," I said when she just stared at me, her brows lifted. "It's a Bloody Mary."

She snorted.

"Sex on the Beach?"

Pretty brown eyes rolled.

"Rum and Coke?"

Anabelle set the glass down into the rack, moved on to the next, not even bothering to acknowledge that guess.

"I've got it!" I said, loving that her focus arrowed back to mine.

"Okay, Sherlock," she said. "What is it?"

"A virgin daiquiri."

My only response was a slow shake of her head, but I could have sworn as she turned away to stash the glasses that her lips had tipped up just the slightest bit at the edges.

Progress.

Still didn't completely understand why I was so desperate for that progress, but considering my attraction to her was the first emotion aside from guilt that I'd felt in far too many years, I was going with it.

"Does anyone ever call you Belle?"

Shoulders gone stiff, a slow swivel back, a dark glare. "No."

Said so absolutely that it would have taken an idiot to not see that I was treading in dangerous territory.

"Not a fan?"

"Considering I'm not a Disney princess," she said archly, "no."

"But you like reading, right?" Brooke asked. "Like the real Belle?"

I'd felt my sister approaching, had seen her trademark red hair in the mirror, so I didn't startle.

Anabelle did, however, and I'd be lying if I said seeing her so focused on our conversation didn't call to something primitive inside me.

Mine.

Even though I had absolutely no right.

"Not sure there *is* a real Belle," Anabelle muttered. "But, yes, I like reading just fine."

"Just fine?" A gasp, Brooke clasping her hands to her chest. "You wound me."

I chuckled, nudged her with my shoulder. She'd always been a melodramatic little thing, and I loved her for it. "Hey, little sis," I said, forcing my gaze from the *prickly* little thing in front of me to the little thing I was related to.

And, yes, I knew full well that both women would like to be referred to as *little things* about as much as they would appreciate their favorite reality show being canceled.

Two days home and I'd already been introduced to TLC and all the "gloriousness" (Brookie's words, not mine) of their reality TV lineup.

"Hey, big bro," she said. "Or should I say, *older by ten minutes,* bro."

"Watch it." I nudged her again, this time with my elbow, but I couldn't hold back my smile. "Missed you, kid."

Those emerald eyes shone. "No emotions," she ordered. "I just wrote a very sad scene, and I'm on edge."

Iris gasped as she slid onto the stool on the other side of me.

I'd met Brent's fiancé officially earlier that evening and though my best friend was still keeping his distance—in fact, he'd barely said five more words to me—his woman hadn't done the same.

She'd marched right up to me, grasped both my arms, and said, "You made a mistake, but you're here. You're family." A squeeze before she let go and stepped back, voice dropping. "He'll forgive you. Just be patient."

In the present, however, Iris didn't appear the least bit patient. Her gaze was greedy, her tone demanding. "Tell me you did *not* kill off Chase."

Brooke's smile went decidedly evil.

There was no other way to describe it.

Her words matched. "You know an author never tells."

Iris moaned, pressed her hands to her cheeks. "Oh, no. Please, no. He's mine." Accusing eyes directed at Brooke. "You promised."

"I thought *I* was yours." Soft words, male words. A tenderness in my best friend's—or the man who *had* been my best friend before I'd ruined our relationship—voice I'd never thought I would hear.

Tough had melted, transformed into devotion, to love, to—

Fuck.

I shouldn't have spent the last few months reading my sister's books. I'd wanted to catch up on her life, make sure I hadn't missed anything important that might not have been highlighted in the surveillance. Also—and I was fully aware this made me sound like a complete asshole—but I'd never bothered to read them before, thinking they were boring and sappy and . . . not good.

See?

Asshole.

But I'd read the first one and been hooked.

She wrote about vulnerable heroes and heroines and did it in a way that was realistic and heartfelt.

And I was so damned proud of her.

My sister was talented.

However, now as acute longing coursed through me, I realized that bingeing all of her books over a few short months had flipped some sort of switch in me. I was turning into an utter romantic, one whose throat got a little tight when I heard my friend talking to his woman in that gentle tone.

He loved her, plain as day.

And I was happy for him.

But . . . it was also a reminder of everything I had left behind. Everything I'd missed out on finding.

So . . . *fuck.*

I shifted, my eyes meeting Brent's as he wrapped his arm around Iris's shoulders, tugged her into his side. But our gazes only locked for a moment because she was already turning into him, wrapping her arms around his waist and hugging him tight.

"Ready to go, baby?" she asked, the question punctuated by a yawn.

"All set."

Blue-green eyes narrowed in my sister's direction. "If you killed off Chase, he'd better have a resurrection."

Brooke finger-waved.

Iris made a face.

Then Brent kissed her temple, whispered something in her ear that had red streaking across her cheekbones, and they hightailed it out of the bar.

My sister sighed. "That's romance. Off the pages. Tangible and real-life." She smiled. "I'm so glad he found her."

"Me, too," I agreed.

And though it was true, I had to work really fucking hard to keep any trace of jealously out of my voice. I wanted that—

someone to know every part of me, the flaws, the good things, the really fucking bad, and to still love me at the end of it.

Of course, Brent didn't have bad parts.

I'd known him long enough to recognize that. He was a good guy with a big heart, who'd put his life on the line for this country. Brent was a hero. Full stop.

I was . . .

Complicated.

I'd served. I'd sacrificed. I'd put my life on the line.

But I wouldn't call myself good. Not with the deceit, not when I'd left my friends on to fight alone on a dusty battlefield. Not—

"Get out of here."

Anabelle's voice drew me out of the memories, and I looked up to see that Kace had come up to stand next to her, towel thrown over one shoulder.

"I'll lock up," she said. "Brooke looks ready to fall asleep on her feet. The three of you should get home."

My eyes flicked to the left, and I made the instant judgment that Brooke didn't look tired in the least. My eyes flicked back to the front in time to see Kace scowl. "I'm not leaving you here by yourself."

"I'll be fine." A beat. "Plus, I have tomorrow night off. I'll make sure everything is good to go and then head back to my place to crash."

"Anabelle—"

"I have my car. I'm not a child."

Kace opened his mouth.

I took advantage of what was most certainly going to be a stalemate for my own benefit. "I'll stay with her," I interjected.

Three gazes shot toward me.

I shrugged. "I'm still off on my sleep schedule." My eyes moved to Kace's, held. "I'll hang out, make sure she gets to her car, and then take the *long* way and walk back to you guys' place."

Brooke cocked her head to the side, brows drawn together.

But Kace merely smiled. He knew what I meant, and I was ruthlessly using the knowledge that I'd invaded their lives with little notice while also determinedly ignoring that I was all but giving this man permission to sleep with my sister.

See?

Not good.

Especially since I had an ulterior motive . . . and she was standing directly across the bar from me.

"Why would you take the long way round?" Brooke asked, way too innocently.

I smothered a grin. "I need the exercise."

"I—" Her mouth opened and closed. "At this time of night? That's dangerous and—"

"He's giving you two love birds time to bone," Anabelle interjected dryly.

Brooke gasped, but she couldn't really work up any amount of outrage, not when Kace had gathered her things, rounded the bar, and was herding her off the stool and out of the building in all of a minute.

Then it was just me . . . and Anabelle.

"Okay," she said, tossing down the towel she'd been drying a glass with. "Now it's time for you to go."

I frowned.

She waved her hand in the direction of my face. "Put the scowl away. I didn't make a fuss because I don't need Kace here to close down," she said. "But I also definitely don't need you here."

Always a fight. Always so tough.

I knew I wouldn't win an argument with her, so I just shrugged and said, "I know."

One eyebrow arched up. "You *know?*" she asked, and it was a dangerous question.

"Yup." I leaned one elbow on the bar, smiled at her.

"And what?" she asked, plunking her hands on her hips. "You're just going to stay right there?"

"Yup," I said again.

She sighed, closed her eyes for a long moment then opened them, fixing me in place. "There's no point in arguing, is there?"

"Nope."

A beat before she hit me with a curveball I knew was designed to make me run. But I'd spent years in terrifying situations, years putting my life on the line. I wasn't that weak.

Even though the question was a fucking doozy.

"You really don't care that your sister is having sex?"

I stifled a shudder . . . along with the urge to go hunt down Kace, no matter that I'd just given him carte blanche. The truth was that I hated it, so fucking much, and knew I'd never think anyone was good enough for her. But—

"She's a grown woman," I said, telling the truth, as much as it pained me. "She's allowed to make her own decisions, allowed to be the one to figure out who she's letting into her life, her body." I shrugged, feeling far less casual than my words dictated. Because even though it went against every protective bone in my body, Brooke didn't answer to anyone but herself. "She deserves to find her happy ending," I told Anabelle. "And frankly, after everything she went through, she deserves to have a man who looks at her like Kace does."

Silence.

Then, "He does look at her right." She nodded, tossed her towel down, then slipped out from behind the bar. "So, the *long* way round?" Her lips twitched.

This time I did shudder. But, pushing the thoughts of Kace

and my sister doing whatever they were going to do for the *long* way round, I got up from the stool and moved toward Anabelle.

She grinned, led the way into the hallway. "Men. Always feeling the need to be so protective."

"Look who's talking," I teased. "You've got protective down pat."

A roll of deep brown eyes. "I look out for the people who belong to me."

"*Belong* to you?"

"Yup." A shrug as she put in a code above the doorknob then pushed open the wooden panel. A different door than the other night, this one had a label in the center of it that read "Office." She stepped in and reappeared a second later, a plain black backpack in her hand. "They pulled me into their little circle of happy," she said, shrugging into it and closing the door behind her, "so now they have to put up with my snarky, ill-tempered ass."

"I happen to think that snarky and ill-tempered is sexy."

She huffed out a breath. "You're just pent up." She strode out into the front room of Bobby's. A large open area with another bar, this one tended to cater to a younger, more college-aged crowd. The back room, where I'd spent my time, where Kace, Anabelle, and Brent worked, was quieter, filled with fewer frat boys and more young professionals.

Different vibe.

Chiller vibe.

Obviously, I preferred the back room. Absence of twenty-somethings aside, it was where the cool kids hung out.

Anabelle crossed the space, checked that the front door was locked, then hit some buttons on a keypad behind the bar. I trailed her back out as I heard the security system begin the countdown to arm itself.

Breasts bouncing, ass swaying. God, I could watch her stride around purposefully for *days*.

"Come on," she snapped, not stopping as she glared at me over her shoulder.

Or not.

I got my ass into gear, followed her out of the front room, down the hall, and out the back door.

She pushed out, not holding it for me, but I didn't mind.

I'd seen her play nice that evening with almost every customer, aside from one who'd been a total jerk to his girl-friend. *He'd* gotten the icy glare, his drink deliberately forgotten for long minutes.

Part of me knew that she wasn't playing nice with me, not like she had the majority of the customers. Another part knew she wasn't just ignoring me like the other peons who'd failed to gain more than a passing awareness from her that evening— passing because she'd served them, failure because she'd paid no notice to them otherwise. So, she wasn't ignoring me, and she definitely wasn't playing nice. Therefore, I was hedging my bets in the belief that she must be feeling this strange draw just the same as me.

Either that, or she just doesn't like your dumb ass, and is putting up with you for Brooke's sake, my mind chimed in helpfully.

There was that.

She was attached to my sister, to Brooke and Kace and Iris.

She'd called them family.

I didn't move as she leaned in to check the door had latched, and consequently, didn't miss her breath catch when she got close enough to scent.

My inhaling that spicy floral scent had her freezing, had her head turning, eyes locking with mine. "Did you seriously just smell me?" she asked, completely aghast. The deep brown of her irises was almost black in the dim light.

I shrugged. "You smell good."

"I—" A shake of her head. "Smell—" Another. "You've lost it, you know that, right?"

"Will you think I've lost it if I tell you you're the first woman I've wanted in years?"

She snorted, started walking toward a silver sedan. "Um, yes."

"Why?"

A dark glare over her shoulder. "Um . . . because you're you and I'm me."

I frowned. I'd already told her she was the sexiest woman I'd ever laid eyes on. I hadn't been lying. "What does that mean?"

"Come on," she said with a gloomy laugh. "You had to have seen the girls looking at you tonight. You could have had any one of them in bed in an instant, no sweet-talking needed."

I hadn't been paying attention to other girls. I'd been salivating over *her*. "Would you come to my bed if I sweet-talked *you?*"

She pulled out her keys, bleeped the locks. "No."

"No?"

"Nope."

She yanked open the door, stopped when I asked, "Why not? Am I not pretty enough for you?"

Anabelle snorted. "You're joking, right? You're pretty much the most attractive man that I've ever seen."

There were parts of that I liked—*the most attractive man I've ever seen.*

And there were parts I despised—*pretty much.*

"What?" I asked. "You like the guys who were desperate to get your attention all night better? The ones who were all but begging you for their chance to sweet-talk you into *their* bed?"

Her fingers clenched on the frame of the door. "You're insane. No one even gave me a second look." She started to get in the car.

Delusional. As in, this woman was completely delusional. But the other guys didn't matter, didn't play into this. Because, "I did."

She stopped, glanced up at me. "What?"

"I gave you a second look and a third and a—"

A roll of her eyes. "*Sure,* you did."

"Why don't you believe me?" I asked, stepping closer. "And don't give me any bullshit about you saying that you're not attractive. You're a strong, modern woman, and you know that shines through."

Except . . . was that a slice of vulnerability in her eyes?

It was hard to tell, the glow from the moon was diffused through several layers of clouds and the interior light in her car not doing much to illuminate her face.

"Yup," she said after a moment. "That's me. I'm confident and strong and that adds to my mantle as the sexiest woman you've ever seen. I'm more gorgeous than a supermodel. I'm hotter than a Playboy spread. I—"

I ran the back of my knuckles over her cheek.

The sarcasm was strong with this one.

"I know you're not fishing for compliments," I said. "But I'm going to give them to you anyway." I brushed my thumb along her bottom lip. "This mouth had me waking up hard as a rock this morning, imaging what it might taste like." I stroked my finger across one collarbone then the other. "These I want to trace my tongue across, dip lower"—I slid that finger just beneath the collar of the pale pink sweater she was wearing—"and this"— I skated my hand down her side, played my fingers mere millimeters from her luscious ass—"I want to take a bite out of."

Her breath shuddered out, her head shook in disagreement. "We won't have any chemistry. I know it."

More lies. But rather than calling her on the fact that I could almost scent her desire, could see that her nipples had hardened against the fabric of her bra, all but begging to be stroked, I asked, "How do you know it?"

"Because—"

I placed a finger over her lips. "Don't say *because I'm me and you're you*."

She narrowed her eyes, shoved the finger away. "I can say whatever the fuck I want to say. I don't have to prove anything to you and—"

"*That's* why you're the sexiest woman I've ever seen."

"You're impossible." She sighed.

"Maybe," I said and cupped her cheek, allowed myself the barest touch of her lips. So soft under my thumb, so warm and tempting. "But I'm not lying. You're—"

A disgusted noise. "Maybe this will dissuade you," she muttered. "Maybe *this* will make you see reason."

I was frowning, trying to understand what would make me see reason and didn't process her raising onto her tiptoes, didn't fully register her slipping out from behind the car door. Not until her body brushed mine, not until flames erupted below the surface of my skin at the simple contact.

Then her mouth pressed to mine.

And the world exploded.

Or maybe that was just my brain, because the light touch of her lips against mine, her smell drifting over me, the silky softness of her skin under my palm . . . they were nirvana and pain. So fucking good, but also filling me with so much longing that I could barely control the urge to yank her against me and devour her.

But she was giving me light and sweet, and that tempered the raging need that swept over me.

Then her tongue traced the seam of my lips.

I opened and my hand clenched on her waist, drew her close, fingers slipping beneath the sweater to find skin.

More silk. More heat. More . . . *need*.

Forget the hauling her near and devouring her mouth. I wanted her naked and pinned against the car as I thrust home. Or naked and in the back seat. Or naked and on the hood—

I was sensing a theme.

But I wasn't processing much else.

Not when Anabelle's lips were on mine. Not when she tasted like ambrosia and sin and temptation. Not when the moment her mouth met mine, the moment her tongue slid into my mouth, the moment her breasts brushed my chest, every other kiss and touch and female disappeared from memory.

There was before.

And there was Anabelle.

She pushed against my chest, a rough bit of contact that made me want to clutch her tighter, but I forced my hands to release, forced myself to let her draw back.

Her gaze fell to the pavement and stayed there for a long moment.

Then she drew in a deep, slow breath, released it just as slowly.

"There," she said, the words cool, her demeanor calm and collected. "You see? Nothing to write home about. Find another female to quench your need."

I grabbed her arm. "Anabelle."

She yanked herself free. *"Don't."* She glared at me when I went to reach for her again, and I forced my arms to drop to my side even though I wasn't sure if the rejection, the sharp tone was from the nickname or the touching.

Maybe both.

Because she sidled back, got into her car, and started to shut the door. "Enjoy the long way round," she said just before it closed.

The engine started up.

She backed her car out of the spot.

Then she was gone, taillights fading in the distance.

I began walking back to Brooke and Kace's place.

For the record, I did not enjoy the long way round.

And I definitely didn't enjoy it long enough because when I let myself into the apartment, I was greeted with the sound of my sister's giggles, of a low male voice encouraging her to, "*Move*, baby."

On second thought, I shut the door, locked it, and took another lap.

I WAS STANDING on a familiar front porch, debating whether to knock and potentially have Brent ignore me or to just wait until he came out.

The man would need to leave at some point, right?

Except, I'd been sitting in my car for nearly an hour, then on the porch for almost twenty minutes.

Any longer and someone was going to call the police and report me.

But just as I lifted my hand to knock, the door flew open and Brent stood on the threshold, eyes cold, arms crossed.

"You going to case out my house all day?" he snapped.

"No, I—"

"That something they taught you at KTS?" Another terse question.

"Getting caught waffling about knocking on someone's

porch?" I muttered. "No. Patience while I figured out my next move? Yes."

Brent didn't unfreeze in the least, but I'd known my friend long enough to detect a modicum of that ice surrounding him melting.

"I guess they taught you that," Brent snapped, "along with pretending to have PTSD and mental health issues, which contributed to your death?"

Or not.

I sighed, leaned back against one of the pillars. "The PTSD was real. *Is* real."

Silence, then, "Did you get help for it?"

"Yeah." I nodded. "Never completely goes away though."

He uncrossed his arms, ran a hand over his hand, and I saw the same haunted look in his eyes that I knew was sometimes in mine. "No, it doesn't."

"It was a mistake to join up with KTS. I knew it as soon as they said I needed to disappear. But . . . I was fucking stubborn and I thought I was going somewhere I could make a difference, to do something to help without all the rules and regulations we had dealt with while deployed." I sighed. "Found out pretty quickly that no place is perfect, least of all one that was sold as a hero's utopia."

"If I remember correctly, I told you that."

"Yes, you did."

"But you went anyway."

"I did. And I *did* help. It just . . . wasn't the payoff I'd expected."

"And you hurt Brooke," he said, eyes flashing. "She was devastated after your death, or rather, your *fake* death, or what-ever the fuck it was."

"She wasn't the only one I hurt," I said and held his gaze. "I'm sorry. I should have listened to you in the first place, should have never gone along with their plan when I found out what they wanted to do."

Brent nodded, and for a moment, I thought he'd let me in a little.

Instead, he stepped back, fingers going to the panel of the door, eyes cold. "You have a lot to make up for."

Then the door closed, and I was alone.

SEVEN

Anabelle

I'D BEEN SLEEPING for all of an hour when my cell rang.

My eyes flicked to the window, and I saw it was still dark, the sun just barely beginning to transform the black and navy of the middle of the night into what would be the crimsons, and oranges, and yellows of the early morning.

At that moment, the sky was dark, the hills in the distance outlined with the faintest glow.

And I knew who would be calling.

Sighing, I reached over and picked up my phone.

"Dad Calling" was on the screen.

Exactly as I suspected. Groaning, I dropped it to the mattress and debated between answering it and letting it go to voicemail. My dad just couldn't let it go, not even after I'd made my wishes crystal clear. He'd push and press, get my siblings on his side to turn the bolts on their end.

The only thing was that I was the baby.

The youngest child.

I'd gotten off easy, according to my siblings—had rules that were less strict, a curfew that was a whole hour later, and I'd even been able to have a boyfriend.

But it was hard living in the shadow of my siblings.

A rocket scientist and a CEO.

Ivy league schools and 4.0s.

Never pushing the limits, always making things easier on my parents.

And . . . I worked in a bar. Was a college dropout. I didn't miss school, didn't regret leaving. I'd learned more about myself traveling around the world, experiencing different countries, different lives.

I'd started in the Philippines, had seen my grandmother for the third time in my life.

Growing up, I hadn't made too many trips to the country my mom was from. Plane tickets got infinitely more expensive the more kids someone had—funny that. Add in trips to South Korea to visit my dad's family, my parents saving for those expensive colleges they expected us to attend, and a whole host of extracurriculars, and there just hadn't been too many international vacations.

Twice.

Once when I was a baby to meet my mom's family—which I obviously didn't remember.

And a second time, when my aunt had died, barely a year before my mom was gone. Two sisters, both taken too soon by cancer. There were some holes that were never filled, and my grandmother knew that.

Too old to make the trip to the States, I was infinitely glad that the first ticket I'd booked after dropping out of school had been to see her.

Especially since she was gone now.

Another hole.

Sighing, I ignored the persistent buzzing and thought about the request my father had made for me to move to the East Coast.

I liked my life here. I could be myself, not some buffed and polished version I felt necessary to show my dad, my siblings, trying unsuccessfully to prove to them and myself that I *could* fit in if I cared enough to try.

Except . . . I'd spent my whole life trying to fit in.

And I'd spent exactly the same amount of time feeling like I never could.

Here, with Brooke, Kace, Iris, and Brent, they didn't care that I'd only just finally saved up enough money to afford to purchase a car for the first time in my life—and they certainly didn't care that I hadn't been able to splurge for leather seats or a backup camera.

Instead, Brooke had bought me a unicorn to perch on my dashboard—her joke that I was like the mythical creature because I could gore a bitch with my horn much more easily than I farted rainbows. Kace and Brent had painted a special parking spot for me out back, emblazoning the end with "Reserved for Anabelle." Iris had baked her special sugar cookies, cut in the shape of tiny cars and painted silver to match mine.

On the other hand, my father, for all that I knew he loved me, had said, "You've purchased your *first* car?" when I told him how excited I was.

I should have known better.

My siblings drove Range Rovers.

I had a Toyota.

A fine car, a *great* car I was thrilled to have.

But it wasn't a Range Rover or a Lexus or a Mercedes.

It was average, and Kims did not do average.

"Enough," I muttered. I'd made the choice a long time ago that I was going to live my own life, doing what made me happy.

Brent and Iris, Kace and Brooke, Bobby's, my car, my tiny cottage. The ocean forty-five minutes away. The mountains three and a half hours the other direction. Warm spring mornings. No snow. Air that was clean and easy to breathe. Safe streets to walk. Reliable power and water. Millenia old redwoods in lieu of thousand-year-old ruins. Netflix and sleeping in. Going to the movies by myself and eating a gallon of popcorn.

Those were the things that made me happy.

A simple life. Needs fulfilled, joy in the details.

I'd learned just how lucky I was during my travels.

And I wasn't ready to give up my lucky. No matter that someone else didn't see the blessing in it. Not now. Not *ever*.

But . . . the last time my dad had pressed this hard, I'd had to leave the country to find some peace. I'd enjoyed it, obviously. Had spent those years abroad, working odd jobs, and navigating the visa requirements with the same sort of focused studied I'd once saved for studying mathematical equations.

Yes, an Asian who loved math. Just let the clichés run wild.

But while math had come easy, it wasn't all that I was. I'd loved English, had spent too many hours devouring book upon book upon book. I'd visited libraries just as often as I'd visited museums.

I wrinkled my nose.

Fuck, I guess that was another stereotype.

Anyway, my point was, I'd been a good kid, from a good family, attending a good school, getting good grades.

Until it was all gone.

Until I hadn't been able to keep doing that.

Now—

My phone buzzed again, and I jumped, realizing that in my

half-sleepy, half-memory submerged brain, I'd let the call go to voicemail.

And now it was ringing again.

Yay.

"Hello, Dad," I said, answering it and stifling my annoyance.

"Were you asleep?" he asked. "It's not like a Kim to laze around in bed."

"I'm on Pacific time, remember? It's five in the morning."

"Oh." A beat. "If you moved—"

I bit back my sigh. Ten seconds? Maybe, five. As in, it had taken him all of five seconds to bring up the topic of the move.

"I love you, Dad. But I'm staying here."

Silence.

"Please, don't push me," I said. "I'm happy. I have a good job, great friends. A nice place to live."

"This good job is working in a bar," he reminded me. "That's not exactly what your mother or I wanted for you." A low blow, bringing my mom into the conversation so early. Usually, he waited a bit longer to bring in the big guns. Which meant he was either getting desperate, or he'd decided to stop playing nice. "And you're not going to know your nieces and nephews if you keep working at this bar and don't come home."

"I grew up here, Dad," I said. "It feels more like home than anywhere I've visited."

He ignored the truth in that statement and said, "You didn't even visit us for Christmas."

That was true. But I hadn't gone home for two reasons. One, I hadn't wanted to get the in-person guilt trip from my father about moving. Two, because flights to the East Coast at Christmas time were very expensive. And after buying my car— outright, thank me very much—I hadn't had enough for a flight to visit my family.

I *had* shipped presents to my siblings' houses, spending an exorbitant amount on both adorable onesies for my new niece and dinosaur action figures for my nephews, along with items for my dad, my brother and sister, and their spouses. And that wasn't even including the cost of shipping that giant ass box of gifts or the amount of time I'd spent wrapping the gifts.

Let it be known, animatronic T-Rexes that roared and toddled made for very difficult wrapping.

"I had to work," I said, sticking with my lie. "And I know Kelly and Tom got the gifts. They sent loads of pictures of the baby in the outfits I picked out and the kiddos playing with the dinosaurs."

"What kind of bar is open on Christmas?"

"Not everyone celebrates the holiday, Dad."

Silence.

"I don't like it."

"I know." A beat. "But I'm not moving. I'll get a few days off soon and will come visit."

More silence.

"I promise." When he didn't say anything further, just radiated disapproval through the airwaves, I sighed. "I have a lot to do today. I love you and will talk to you soon, okay?"

Another long pause before he said, "Okay."

That was it.

Just okay.

I knew I wouldn't get anything more from him, no affection or soft words—that had been my mom's job—but having that knowledge didn't mean it hurt any less. Sadness sliced through me, chased just as quickly with longing. I missed my mom. I missed the family unit we'd been when she was alive.

But she was gone.

And things would never go back to the way they'd been before.

Heart heavy, just as it always was after these conversations,

I said goodbye, hung up, and leaned over to my nightstand so I could plug my phone back in.

Then I got back to my *a lot to do.*

I pulled the blankets over my head and went back to sleep.

Because sometimes it was easier to be unconscious than to deal with reality.

EIGHT

Hayden

"SPILL."

It was just after eleven in the morning and I glanced up at my twin, her hair a mess, sleep still in her eyes, but her expression mulish.

And I knew I wouldn't get away with the half-explanation I'd given her on Christmas.

Didn't mean I wasn't going to try to get out of this conversation. Brooke didn't need to shoulder my guilt, didn't need to help me talk out the tangle of my thoughts.

She deserved to live her life without my complications.

Which was why I played stupid and said, "Spill what?"

No response, and for a second, I thought that she'd actually let it go, that she'd taken my explanation at face value and would let us move on.

Then I heard the stool next to me creak as she sat down on it.

"You pretended to have committed suicide, Hayden." Her voice was quiet and trembled. "I had to identify your body."

She didn't ask the question outright, but I told her the answer anyway. She *had* "identified" me, had gone through hell and back. If she wanted it, she deserved as much of the truth as I could give her.

"I was drugged," I said, "and the medical examiner was one of us."

"I figured as much when you said they arranged it." Her eyes fell to her lap. "I guess, the bigger question is 'who are *they?*'"

"I can't tell you that, Brookie," I admitted. "I wish I could, and maybe even a year ago I would have said they recruited me because they thought that only I could help." I shrugged. "But the truth is that while I have an aptitude with hacking, with technology, especially under duress and in the field, plenty of other guys do too."

"So . . . why you?" A soft question, but with unvarnished pain that made my guilt pulse anew.

"I think they understood I was vulnerable. I met Daniel at a bar while on leave." I shook my head, remembering how lost I'd been, how desperate I was to convince myself of the fact that I was a fucking hero. "I missed Mom and Dad, missed you, and day in and day out it was the same thing. Following commands I didn't believe in—not from Brent, he always had our back—but from the top down, things over there were a shitshow and we weren't making one bit of difference. Or . . . at least it felt that way."

"You always wanted to be a hero," Brooke murmured. "You were always the good guy in our pretend game, hated books and movies where the bad guys won." She touched my arm. "You wanted to help."

Pipe dreams, but, "Yeah."

She dropped her hand into her lap. "So, you felt like you

weren't making a difference and these guys gave you what? Like a job offer but for private military services?"

I nodded. "Sort of. They work with the government, so it's not like I'm going to get court-martialed or face repercussions now that I'm alive again. My record was classified, the change in position noted, but the group is off the map, independently run, and supposed to be that final barrier between the bad guys and civilians."

A pause then, "Brent didn't seem to believe that."

"No," I admitted. "I introduced him to Daniel when they made the offer, thought we could go in together—" The flare of pain in her eyes had me reaching over and squeezing her hand. "I didn't know then that I'd have to be erased. I'm sorry."

Green eyes on mine, holding for several long moments. "I know you are," she whispered before adding in a more normal tone, "I'm guessing the meeting didn't go well?"

I shook my head. "Brent said he had a bad feeling about the guy, and I pretended to agree."

"But you didn't?"

"I don't know if I did or I didn't," I said and sighed. "I think I was too wrapped up in the excitement of it. They needed me. This super cool, covert group that was filled with badasses needed *me*." I clenched my hands into fists. "My ego was stroked, and I kept meeting with Daniel. Eventually, after the explosion and Brent was hurt, after we lost our friends . . . I figured I didn't have anything else to lose and decided to join up."

She nodded, but the hurt was still in her eyes, in the careful way she held herself.

Unable to see the person who'd been my other half, who was still ingrained so deeply inside my heart, hurting, I wrapped my arm around her. "I'm sorry, Brookie, if I'd known then . . ."

She didn't answer, but her arms convulsed, and she held me

tight for a long moment. Then she pulled back. "I can't say that I understand fully," she whispered. "I can't say I quite forgive you yet. But I know you made the choice you had to and what I said the other day stands true. I'm glad you're back." She nudged my shoulder with hers. "I know what's it like to have a life without you. I don't want that again."

"Even if I'm not exactly the same?" I couldn't help asking.

"Newsflash," she said, lips curving. "It's been ten years. I'm not the same either."

"True. But I hear ugliness is a slowly progressing condition," I teased.

Brooke smacked me and jumped off her stool, heading for the coffee pot and pouring herself a cup. "I hear the same thing about baldness."

I narrowed my eyes, hand instinctively lifting to my head. Our dad had been bald.

She smirked, set down her mug.

"Brat."

"Takes one to know—*Hayden!*"

I'd moved.

Closing the distance between us and scooping her off her feet, fingers finding all of those ticklish spots I'd learned and honed over the years.

Unfortunately, my plan wasn't perfect.

Because she knew my ticklish spots, too, and pretty soon we were collapsed on the floor like a couple of ten-year-olds, fingers flying, laughing until tears poured down our cheeks.

I was stronger, but she was wily.

And so we entered a stalemate.

Which was how Kace found us maybe five minutes later, still trying to best one another, though the effort was mostly half-hearted.

"Is this some weird twin thing?" he muttered, stepping over me and pouring himself some coffee.

"Yup," Brooke said, pushing her hair off her face. "Get used to it."

"Heaven help me," Kace muttered and stepped over me again to leave the kitchen.

I snorted. Brooke giggled.

Our eyes met, and thirty-plus years of memories passed between us.

"I think you picked good," she whispered.

"What?"

"Anabelle."

My mouth dropped open. "How?"

She touched my cheek. "I saw how you looked at her, and—"

"Brooke," I said, not wanting her to think I can home for any reason but to be here with her, with Brent. "I didn't—"

"Shh," she murmured. "It's not like that at all. I like that you look at her that way. She needs affection and care and someone to love her beyond reason." She brushed back my hair. "And I think Anabelle might fit perfectly into the giant hole you have in your heart."

My breath caught, and I felt the organ expand. My twin was the best.

"You've always loved generously," Brooke murmured, "and she needs that."

I tugged a strand of her hair.

She punched me lightly on the jaw.

"I love you, big bro," she murmured.

"I love you, too, baby sis."

Yeah, it was damned good to be home.

"Do you even own a different type of clothing?" was the pert question that greeted me the moment I sat down on the barstool in Bobby's.

It was late, after eleven, and two nights since I'd "helped" Anabelle with restocking the shelves.

I glanced drown, saw I was wearing cargos and a T-shirt, along with boots.

Same as I wore every day.

A glass plunked in front of me, a beer drawn off the tap with the perfect amount of head, because while I'd not been able to guess Anabelle's favorite drink, she apparently knew what type of beer I liked. My eyes drifted back up, saw she'd already moved away, was talking to a customer a few stools down.

She nodded, lips curved up just at the corners, and turned away, scooping up ice and measuring out alcohol into a shaker with calm, assured movements.

Smooth, graceful, confident.

Yeah, that was sexy.

Perhaps even sexier than the kiss she'd laid on me two nights before, trying to *dissuade* me.

Instead, it had only increased my growing desire until it swirled within me at a fever pitch. I'd woken with a hard-on yesterday morning, and that was something I really wasn't into, not when the couch I'd woken up on with said hard-on belonged to my sister.

So, I'd gone house hunting.

One of the few positives in my time working for KTS was that they paid well. My military days had been much less lucra-tive, but my ten years in the private company meant that I had a nice nest egg and could afford to buy a house near Brooke.

Nothing extravagant, and with my budget it would probably be a fixer-upper, but it would be a place to call home.

And I didn't mind working with my hands.

Especially as I tried to figure out what I wanted to do with my life now that I was out.

"Refill?"

I blinked, glanced from my empty glass up to Anabelle.

She seemed impatient, annoyed at having to serve me . . . except for the trace of heat in those dark brown eyes.

Yeah, her kiss had done about as much to dissuade her as it did to dissuade me.

I grinned. "Screwdriver," I said confidently, though I knew sure as hell that wasn't right. It was getting more and more fun to pull out the most ridiculous suggestions, just to see outrage flit across that beautiful face.

And right on cue, she gasped. "How dare you?"

I chuckled, pushed my glass toward her. "Another beer, please."

Narrowed eyes, pursed lips . . . and I couldn't help myself.

Stretching up, I leaned across the bar top and dropped my voice in the vicinity of bedroom. "Fuck, you're making me want to kiss you again."

Anabelle leaned back, a muscle in her jaw twitching. "If you remember correctly, I kissed *you*."

I relaxed on the stool, let my smile come up slowly, allowed the need this woman had somehow turned into a maelstrom to bleed into my tone. "I remember, Rocky."

"Rocky?"

"Yeah," I said. "Rocky." I flashed a grin. "Because you go into every conversation with me like it's a battle." A beat. "Or boxing match." I winked.

Somehow her glare intensified.

I wouldn't have thought it possible, but she managed to make that glare even . . . glare-ier.

Gold star for the day. I had *all* the grammar and irritation skills.

And maybe some would say it was ill-advised to be provoking the woman I wanted to sweet-talk into bed, but I was sticking with the notion that she couldn't ignore me if she was pissed at me.

So—I bit back a grin when she deposited another beer in front of me, this time with enough force to slosh some of the liquid over the rim of the glass—winning.

"There's your battle," she muttered. "Enjoy your spoils." She spun away.

"Belle?"

A slow turn back, both eyebrows raised. "Belle. Rocky. Is it impossible for you to use my real name?"

"Yes."

She sighed, shook her head.

"I don't have any other clothes."

Her gaze flicked down the half of my body she could see then back up. "Sounds like someone needs to go shopping."

"I hate shopping."

A superior look filled her face. "You still have to go and get it taken care of."

"Come with me."

Superior faded, in came uncertainty. "I—Um. *What?*"

"Yes?"

Brows furrowed, lips parted. "Yes?" she repeated, question in her eyes.

Gotcha. "Great," I said, wrapping my fingers around the beer glass and lifting it up from the bar. "Thanks in advance." I stood. "I'll pick you up tomorrow about two."

Then I ran over to Brooke, firmly inserting myself into the conversation she was having with Iris. My sister glanced at me, at Anabelle, and her eyes asked me the question she didn't allow to cross her lips.

I didn't verbalize my answer, just assured her with *my* eyes that I'd explain later.

A slight nod that was paired with a firm glare, and I knew she'd hold me to that.

Meanwhile, I took the opportunity of the cover to make sure Anabelle couldn't corner me, couldn't find the occasion to tell me in no uncertain terms that she had most certainly not agreed to a shopping venture with me the following day. It wasn't a retreat. More a tactical withdrawal, as was me waiting until Anabelle was distracted by a customer before finishing the beer, leaving some money with Brooke ('cause gotta tip my bartender), and then GTFOing the bar.

I'd get her address from Brooke later. After the explanation, I was certain.

She'd make me bare everything I was feeling, and since she'd accepted my limited explanation about KTS, given her approval of me pursuing something with Anabelle, I knew she'd be ravenous for any and all information I was able to share.

My love life—or lack of it—would be well within her wheelhouse.

But then again, I'd *get* several hours alone with the beautiful Anabelle. So, sharing might not be the worst thing in the world.

There was only one problem.

I hadn't been lying.

I really hated shopping.

———

LATER THAT NIGHT, I dropped the mug of tea next to Brooke's computer, hesitated.

Her fingers barely stopped moving on the keyboard. "What do you want?"

"Nothing," I said, playing innocent.

As anticipated, she saw right through the act.

A sigh, a few more clicks as she finished her sentence, and then she turned to me, arms crossed. "*Hay*," she warned.

"What's Anabelle's address?"

Brows raised, she lifted the mug I'd brought to her lips. "Why?"

"No reason."

"Hmm."

I shifted impatiently from foot to foot, wanting to wait Brooke out, but also knowing that I needed the address more. "Fine," I said. "You know I like her."

Sparks of amusement in those green eyes. "*Like* her like her?

"What, are we sixteen?"

"I'm not going to pass her a note with checkboxes for yes and no over the bar, asking if she likes you back," Brooke said.

"Well, I'm not writing one of those notes with the check-boxes in the first place, so I think we're good."

Brooke grinned. "Phew." A beat and she pretended to wipe sweat off her forehead. "So, what's your plan? To just show up on her front porch and beg her to go on a date with you?" She chuckled. "I can just see you with a boombox, a la *Say Anything*."

"First, I love that movie," I said, "so, no teasing. Second, she's taking me shopping."

"*She's* taking *you* shopping?" Brooke exclaimed, jumping to her feet. "But she hates shopping."

I grinned this time. "I kind of coerced her into it."

"Good."

Surprised, I tilted my head to the side, studying my sister. Anabelle was her friend, shouldn't she be protecting her?

"She needs to be pushed outside of her comfortable box," Brooke said. "And we both know that you can be plenty pushy."

I acknowledged that with a shrug. It was true.

Brooke put her hand on my arm. "Anabelle comes off as really tough and strong, and she is in a lot of ways—and I don't know too much because she's not often inclined to share—but her family . . . I think they hurt her deeply."

"You don't know how?" I asked.

"No," Brooke said. "I've only overheard a few conversations and they seemed . . . tense. And then her expression afterward —" She winced. "There's some pain there. Deep, heavy pain."

Shit. I knew about pain and old wounds, knew that sometimes people needed space for them to heal.

"Should I step back?"

Even just starting to know her, it would hurt like hell. But I didn't want to hurt Anabelle.

"No." Brooke grabbed my arm. "Don't you dare, Hay. She needs someone to not be put off by her sharp edges, needs someone to see the woman she is behind the walls. Because, big bro, she's really awesome." Her fingers tightened. "Not just beautiful and strong, but loyal and thoughtful and really fucking fun to be with. She'd go toe-to-toe with you in a heartbeat. It would be glorious to see someone hold their own with you, to not melt under the force of those baby blues."

I snorted. "I think you like the idea of her busting my balls a little too much."

"Maybe." A shrug. "But I also think you two would be good for each other."

"Yeah?"

"Yeah."

"So, you going to give me the address?"

She dropped my arm and picked up the mug. "Depends."

"On what?"

"Whether you completed the second half of your usual bribe."

Grinning, I pulled out the chocolate bar I'd bought specially for her. "I only *look* stupid."

She snatched it, tore it open, took a huge bite. "Maybe."

I raised my hands, pretending as though I were going to tickle her again. "*Maybe?*"

She swallowed, backed away slowly. "Okay," she said. "Okay, I give!"

One hand still lifted, I waited for her to give me the address then put it into my cell.

Then just because I was an annoying older brother, I snagged the candy bar and took a big bite.

"Hey!"

Giving her a noogie and handing her the chocolate back, I darted away before she could swat me.

"Love you, baby sis!"

A huff, then, "I love you too, pain in the ass," she grumbled, sitting back down into her chair.

And I knew that I might have missed a lot in the last ten years, but at least that missing had made me appreciate the present so much more.

I was back with my family.

I had some possibilities in my future.

Things were looking up.

NINE

Anabelle

HE WAS EARLY.

I'd planned to make my escape, planned it to the point that I was unlocking my car a full half hour before Hayden had said he was going to pick me up.

And he was leaning against my driver's side door.

I stopped, feet sliding to a halt, wanting to play it off like he'd surprised me and not because my heart had skipped a beat seeing him there.

Wind blowing through his hair, a bit of stubble on his cheeks, eyes covered by aviator shades that were way cooler than anything I could pull off. But the most arresting thing was his smile.

Small, the edges of his mouth just turned up but directed at me.

"Hi, Rocky."

I wanted to melt.

I *couldn't* melt.

"Go away," I said, instead of turning into a pile of mush.

Hayden smiled. "I'm ready for my *Pretty Woman* montage of outfit changes. Where will you take me?"

I glanced down at myself, eyes drifting over *my* usual outfit —sweater, jeans, Converse—and then looked back up. "You realize that I'm the person at Bobby's who has the least amount of fashion sense, right?"

Even Brent and Kace dressed better than me.

I had seven sweaters, seven T-shirts, three pairs of jeans, two black leggings, several hoodies, one winter jacket, and a spare pair of Converse. Aside from enough underwear and socks to get me between laundry days, I lived light.

Years of travel had ingrained that in me.

And working at a bar, I hadn't seen the need to change that. Sweater layered over a T-shirt for a cold day. Just the T-shirt for a warm one. Clean undies and socks, and I was good.

"I don't know." Male fingers on the hem of my sweater where it was just drifting over my wrist. "I think blue is your color."

I shivered. "You're deranged.

A shrug. "Maybe." He smiled, not a small one this time, but one that was hot and slow and sent my pulse skitter-skattering. "But I'm also enjoying your range of different words for crazy. Do you read the thesaurus for fun, or maybe you're interviewing to be my personal one?"

"That doesn't make sense," I said, crossing my arms, both because it *didn't*, but also because I didn't want to look too closely at why being anything personal of Hayden's was so tempting.

"No," he said, "it doesn't."

Okay, then.

I was standing in my driveway, ready to make my escape, but there was a sexy—albeit strange—man between me and that flight.

"I don't have time to go shopping with you today."

"Okay." A shrug. An easy expression.

And silence, where he still didn't move off my car, still didn't do anything except stare at me through those sunglasses. Of course, I couldn't actually see his eyes, not through the dark lenses, but somehow, I could sense that his gaze was on me.

He pushed off the car, came very close. Not quite touching, but I knew if I took a deep breath, then my breasts would brush his chest. My nipples went perky at that very thought, heat coiling through my middle, down into my pussy, moisture pooling, desire swelling fast enough that I actually felt my thighs tremble.

And the man hadn't touched me.

But I'd had his mouth on mine just days before, and my body remembered.

Oh Lord, how it remembered.

Lips demanding but soft, hands clenching on my waist and sending rivulets of need sweeping through my nerves. His tongue had been a hot brand, but his hold . . . that had been more.

He'd held me like he cared.

Even though I knew it was impossible.

I'd thought to convince him I wasn't worth it, that we clearly wouldn't work. For God's sake, the man was more than a foot taller than me—just the logistics of that should have been insurmountable without the aid of several apple crates. But . . . our bodies had closed that distance, our mouths had met, and I'd had the single most erotic experience of my life.

"What were you going to do?" he asked, fingers on the hem of my sweater at my wrist again, only this time slipping beneath to caress the skin.

I struggled to keep my breathing even. It was the barest touch and yet . . .

"Anabelle?"

I blinked. "What?"

"You were leaving," he said, stepping closer, and now I was contending with the feel of my hard nipples brushing over his chest. "Where were you going? Today, when you came out and planned on abandoning me to my shopping quest."

Look. I knew I should push back, knew I should continue being contrary just for self-preservation's sake. This man could break me.

So easily.

But he was also . . . temptation.

So much temptation crammed into a six-foot-plus package, so much temptation that my knees were weak, as was my resolve, *and* my tongue.

"The beach," I blurted.

His eyes flicked down to my sneakers, my jeans, my sweater, up to the cloudy sky, a hint of drizzle in the air. "The beach?"

I narrowed my eyes. "Yes, *the beach.* Why do you care?"

Another shrug, this one careless. "I could go to the beach."

"You—?" I was frowning, the question still on the tip of my tongue when he rounded the car and sat in the passenger's seat. "What—"

The door slammed.

"I—" My mouth opened and closed like a fish. I knew it did, knew it looked ridiculous. And yet, I just stood there like a . . . fish.

Did fish stand?

Was I slowly going insane?

The answers to each of those questions were both an affirmative and a negative. I was going to let the universe guess which answer belonged to which question. Although, I was slowly going insane, so really, I supposed I didn't need to leave it to the universe.

Snorting at my idiocy, I debated my options.

I could call Brooke. Demand she come yank her brother out of my front yard, preferably by the ear. But he'd gotten my address from someone, and I knew my friends well enough to understand they'd probably looked for a moment to meddle.

They were awesome. I loved them. They enjoyed meddling.

So no, Brooke would probably just ignore my call.

Or worse, say something like, "You should go for it with my gorgeous brother. Wouldn't it be perfect? We'd be sisters!"

Okay. Full disclosure. She would realistically only say the last two.

I was the one lusting after her brother.

Leaning down to glance through the driver's side window, I jumped when I found those sunglasses pushed up on his head, those piercing blue eyes on mine. The color of the ocean.

The ocean I wanted to visit.

The ocean that would, more than likely, remind me of this man.

He smiled. My thighs went to Jell-O.

"Fuck," I muttered, straightening even while I instinctively knew that I was screwed.

Fine. Option two: gird my loins, ignore the attraction that was melting me from the inside out, and use this time to piss Hayden off so much that he realized I was not worth the trouble.

Was I smart enough to know this was unhealthy?

Yes.

Did I care?

No.

Glaring up at the clouds for one long moment, I shoved down the bone-deep attraction, grasped on to reality (that being Hayden was not for me), then yanked open the driver's side door. A second later, I plunked into the seat. A heartbeat after that, I had the keys in the ignition, the engine started up, and we were backing out of the driveway.

"Cute house," he said.

"I actually live in the cottage out back," I told him. "The owners retired recently and are getting ready to put it on the market."

"What does that mean for you?"

I shrugged, a lot more casually than I actually felt. "Hopefully, the new buyers will be cool and want the rental income. Or," I said, still affecting casual, though it was harder to do, especially since, of all the places I'd lived in the world, the small studio behind this medium-sized bungalow just a few blocks from the bar was my favorite. "I'll move."

I'd hate it, though. I loved the main house as much as I did the studio.

Modern but built to reflect the architecture of the area. Clean lines with a craftsman feel. The best part of the entire house? The backyard. So much greenery in what was a typically arid climate. But the marine layer regularly crept into this neighborhood and because of that, the garden was lush. Cute little flower boxes, a winding paved pathway, old growth trees, and an honest-to-God fountain.

Like living in a fairy princess's forest retreat.

"Nice place to have to leave behind."

Yes, it was. But, "I'm good at leaving things behind."

Silence.

A long moment of quiet that wound tighter and tighter. I could feel Hayden staring at me, but I refused to look, refused to do anything except keep my eyes determinedly on the road.

Finally, he asked, "What kind of things do you leave behind?"

My fingers clenched on the steering wheel, and I knew the movement revealed too much, knew it gave this interesting and intense man a glimpse of something I didn't want to. But I still couldn't stop the response, the words from pouring out and filling the space between us. "Same thing as you, I suppose."

His breath caught.

I heard it, the last sound before more silence descended.

Now, I wondered what was worse. His insightful questions, his flirting, or his silence.

All rubbed my skin raw. All made me want to do things I shouldn't—reveal too much, believe that he might want me, and stop the car, take his hand, and ask him if he was okay after everything that happened.

But he wasn't mine.

Wouldn't be mine.

Maybe he could become family?

The niggling thought made me want too much. I loved Brooke and Iris, Brent and Kace, but it was a love that was careful. These people took care with me, with my heart, with my pain. They loved me back, fiercely, had earned my trust over the years.

Hayden hadn't.

And yet . . . he made me feel much more than I was comfortable with.

Because I thought he could slot himself into my family quite easily.

And when things didn't work out between us, it would hurt like hell to lose Brent, Iris, Kace, or Brooke. I wasn't cold enough to think that it wouldn't, wasn't dumb enough to think they'd choose me over Hayden. But I also knew I would survive it. Because I'd lost my mom, because I'd lost my dad, my sister, my brother—in different ways, but the loss was still there.

But . . . a man would occupy a different space in my heart.

I was too self-aware to not acknowledge that, no matter how

much I wanted to stick my head in the sand and pretend it wasn't like that.

Hayden had looked at me on the porch less than a week ago, and I'd been flayed open, spread wide and available for consumption. I was the zombie, he was the brain. I was drawn to the succor and pulled too deep. It would devastate me when he was gone. There would be no going on, going back, no tucking it all down and moving on.

I'd be broken.

I knew that as intrinsically as I knew that giving in might be worth it anyway.

He was a once in a lifetime man.

Wild. Sweet. Persistent. Charming. Annoying. Sexy. Intense. Too many things and yet the absolute perfect amount.

But I knew I wasn't a once in a lifetime woman.

And there was the crux of the issue. *That* was why I knew I wouldn't be whole at the end of this.

If you know the ending so easily, my baby, my mom's voice murmured. *Then why are you running so scared?*

"I'm not," I muttered, forgetting myself, feeling Hayden's eyes on my profile again, knowing I sounded unhinged or at least a bit kooky to be talking to myself when another human being was in the car.

But I was good at pretending.

So, I just pretended I hadn't said anything. Pretended he wasn't there next to me. Pretended Hayden wasn't a pulse in my heart, a longing in my soul, a—

Take the hard way, baby. Just this once.

I couldn't.

I can't.

Swallowing hard, I continued with the things I was good at —keeping my eyes on the road, smothering the cravings that would make me vulnerable. The freeway was quiet since it was too early for evening rush hour but too late for morning. Coming back from the coast would be a bitch, but I'd been planning on staying late enough to let the traffic settle.

Except, now I had a companion.

I wondered if I should turn back but discounted the thought the moment it crossed my brain. Likely, the stubborn, sexy man would camp out in my car and refused to move, even if I did drive home.

"And I would sleep in here."

I jumped, knowing I hadn't spoken aloud, but his quiet statement filled with heat and determination said he'd read my thoughts anyway.

"What? Your mystery military group teach you ESP as well as how to rise from the dead?"

"Fire."

I blinked, eyes darting to the right before I caught myself. And no, I was not going to ask him to explain.

"The answer to your question is *you* are made of fire."

"Um, I don't think I asked a question whose answer is fire."

"Okay." A shrug. "So it's the answer to the question you didn't ask aloud, the one that's pinging around in your head, the one that's wondering why I'm interested and pushing this and wanting to know you more."

I frowned. "And it's because I'm made of fire."

"Yes." My brows stayed pulled together and I nearly jumped out of my skin when he brushed his fingertips over my cheek. "Yes," he murmured, "because fire is attractive. Fire is admirable. Yes, because I like women who can hold their own. Yes, because I don't give a shit if you bust my balls all day because that just means I'll be able to kiss your smirk off that gorgeous mouth after you finish teasing me."

I swallowed hard, was quiet for too long.

But those words. Fuck, I liked them so much.

I couldn't like them. It was dangerous and risky and I deliberately changed the topic back to something unimportant. "Brooke says I'd be more likely to gore someone with my horn"—I nodded at the unicorn that was perched on my dashboard—"than to fart rainbows."

A pause, and I thought he'd turn the topic back to fire and all those scary assertions.

"I don't know"—my gaze flicked to his again, saw the edges of his mouth curved into a sexy smile, the amusement in his eyes, and I relaxed—"farting rainbows is a special skill. Only the best in the world have it."

"Is that something your super-special-commando training taught you?"

"Absolutely." His smile went full grin. "Unicorn farts are a highly flammable and volatile substance. Only those with superior training can be trusted with their safekeeping."

I chuckled, totally unable to believe we'd gone from talk of fire to having a conversation about unicorn farts . . . and that I was enjoying it.

"Who are you?" I asked incredulously.

Silence, but then again, I was good at creating it, at helping it descend in a hot, uncomfortable blanket that threatened to stifle everyone and everything around me. Maybe *that* was my superpower. Well, the silencing ability paired with no shortage of caustic remarks and an uncanny ability to push people away.

My amusement faded, my fingers clenched on the steering wheel.

"I'm just Hayden," he said, voice soft, tempting.

My fingers stayed clenched.

"And you're just Anabelle."

Yeah, that was the problem.

"I think you're funny and sexy and beautiful. I want to get to know you better. That's it. No strings or undercurrents—

unless you're thinking of the sexual kind, in which case, yes, I've been dreaming about fucking you since the moment I saw you perform calisthenics on Brent's front porch." He brushed his knuckles over my cheek. "I've woken up hard every morning since you kissed me."

I released a shuddering breath. "That kiss was supposed to make it so you *didn't* like me."

Another brush, this time over the corner of my mouth. "It didn't work."

Heat scorching through my body, I took the turn off for the winding highway that would lead down to my favorite beach. "It doesn't make sense, Hayden."

Still close enough for me to smell, to feel, to . . . want.

He leaned back, and it wasn't a slice of disappointment I felt. It wasn't.

"I know," he said, "that I'm just starting to get to know you, just beginning to understand what's going on in that brain of yours. But . . ."

"But what?" I prompted, unable to stop myself.

I shouldn't care about what he was thinking. And yet . . . I did. Admitting that, even just to my own mind, settled the flutters in my stomach, soothed the whirling mess that had been swarming my insides since the first moment I'd seen Hayden. Despite my attempts to pretend otherwise, I was drawn to this man.

It made no sense.

Life sometimes made no sense.

A piece settled in my heart, the vice on my lungs eased.

"But," he said after a long moment, "you're confident." I felt his eyes on me but didn't glance his way. To do so would reveal too much. I *was* confident in my own skin. I knew who I was . . . and who I wasn't.

That part wasn't the problem.

"You're strong and assured behind the bar, protective of my sister, her friends," he went on. "You don't seem to have any doubts about your abilities or your intelligence, but you are completely clueless when it comes to how that confidence speaks to the rest of the world." A beat. "And especially clueless about how it speaks to the male population."

"I'm not clueless," I muttered, slowing as I navigated several switchback turns in a row.

"You're clueless about how I see you."

I sniffed. "You don't know me."

"I *want* to know you."

"It—"

"—doesn't make sense," he said softly, and this time instead of his fingers brushing my cheeks or my mouth, they captured a strand of my hair. "Like silk," he murmured.

I held my breath as I made it around the final turn, as I pulled into the parking lot, releasing it when I paused at the kiosk, rolled my window down, and waved to the park ranger who knew me on sight by now.

"Make sure you bundle up," Jacob said, the ranger I'd come to know just by the sheer number of times I'd visited this little beach. It had become my happy place, and the thirty-second conversations we had when I came in were just the right amount of social interaction for me. "It's pretty cold out there today." His mouth turned up into a smile. "Oh hey, I was going to see if you wanted to grab dinner after you're done. There's a great little restaurant a few miles down . . ." His eyes flicked over my shoulder, his words trailing off, and he was quiet for a long moment.

After a second, I glanced in that same direction, saw that Hayden was staring at him coldly, and when I looked back, he seemed to force his gaze back to mine. I was beyond confused to see disappointment on the edges of his eyes.

Was it because Hayden was in the car?

He'd mentioned dinner several times before, but I'd always needed to get back.

I'd just thought the invitations were because he was friendly. I peeked out of the corner of my eye at Hayden, saw him lift a brow that seemed to say, "You see?" and I liked the smug expression about as much as I enjoyed feeling like I was on my back foot in this interaction with Jacob.

Was I really that clueless?

Hayden's self-satisfied look and Jacob's disappointment told me that maybe I was.

Shit.

"Okay, well, bye," I said with an awkward wave. "I'll uh . . . see you around." I'd pressed the button for the window before the last syllable crossed my lips and hit the gas before the glass panel *snicked* closed.

Heavy quiet descended as I navigated the nearly empty parking lot and slid into a spot.

Hayden's hand slid from my hair to my nape. "Still think I was talking nonsense?"

"I—"

I didn't get a chance to finish my sentence, which was just as well, since I didn't have any clue as to what I would have said anyway.

What wasn't *as well*—or at least not great for the wall I placed between myself and the rest of the world, and definitely not good for the purposeful distance I had inserted between this man and myself—was the kiss he laid on me.

In fact, that touch of his mouth to mine sliced through the layers of concrete, dulled the sharp edges of barbed wire, and arrowed its way right into my heart.

Uh-oh.

TEN

Hayden

I WAS WINNING.

No shopping.

And now this addictive, intoxicating, arresting woman's mouth was on mine.

My cock had been alternating between a state of perpetual chub and rock-hard from the moment I'd seen her at her place. Incongruously, her sharp words had me gritting my teeth against the urge to get her to pull the car over and show her what they did to my cock. But the vulnerability in her eyes tempered that.

This wasn't a game.

She really didn't realize her appeal.

I wasn't sure if someone had been cruel to her—but I was damn sure going to find out and make them pay if they were—or if she just didn't see herself clearly. Either way, I was going to make her understand.

Yes, I knew that made me an egotistical asshole.

No, I didn't give two shits.

Especially not with her lips pressing against mine, her body melting forward. I slid my hand into her hair, nudging the hair tie free, weaving my fingers into the silken black locks, tilting her head so that her mouth was at the perfect angle as I kissed her gently.

Light. Soft. Coaxing.

She sighed against my lips, hers parting, drifting open.

And I couldn't resist the temptation, couldn't stop from taking what she'd unconsciously offered. I delved my tongue into her mouth, rubbed it against hers, steeled myself against the heat that prickled down my spine, that arrowed toward my cock and made it impossibly harder.

She moaned, shifted closer, and I got lost in the feel of her. I cupped her jaw, felt the softness of her skin, so smooth and delicate when mine was roughened with calluses. I sipped at her mouth, tasted the slight bitter of coffee mixing with the sweetness of her lips, her tongue, and sifted my fingers through her hair, imagined what it would look like when it was draped over my pillow. Then I kissed her until I forgot about everything and everyone else in the world.

I kissed her until the guilt wasn't so heavy.

I kissed her until I could pretend what I'd done wasn't shattering to those who loved me.

But I was also cursing giving in to that temptation of her lips because of the fucking console between us—the hard, plastic corner jabbing me in the stomach when all I wanted was to pull her into my arms and kiss her properly—when she pulled away.

One second, she was back to clutching the steering wheel.

The next, she was out of the car, disappearing down a steep path, her black hair flowing behind her like a cape.

I let her go.

Partly because the keys were in the ignition, her purse at the floor near my feet, her jacket and a blanket slung across the back seat.

But also, partly because I had the boner to end all boners, and if I didn't take this moment to breathe, I was going to chase her down, strip her bare, and get us both arrested for indecent exposure.

That thought tempered my desire, and I took a few seconds to grab everything I thought she would need. Purse off the floorboard, jacket and blanket from the back, cell phone from the cradle . . . just in time to have it buzz as I grasped it. Instinct had my eyes dropping to the screen, reading the message before I could rein in my manners and slide it into Anabelle's purse.

You're disappointing Dad.

I froze, heart clenching. I didn't know who the fuck Tom was but considering he was talking about Anabelle's dad, I, unfortunately, had a sinking feeling.

The phone buzzed again, and I didn't even pretend to have manners this time.

I read that message as it flashed onto the screen.

Are you trying to kill him like you killed Mom?

Red hazed my vision. I heard the phone case creak ominously, and I had to resist the urge to launch it at the windshield. Instead, I sucked in a breath, calmly put it into Anabelle's purse, and tugged the keys from the ignition. A few seconds later, I was out of the car and heading down the path.

It was almost a sheer cliff face. The stairs made of rickety wood, its rope railing not holding up well from the onslaught of the ocean. I could see Anabelle below, her hair whipping around in the wind, the bright blue of her sweater standing out sharply against the tan sand. It didn't take long to make my way to the bottom, but I found myself hesitating at the final stair.

Are you trying to kill him like you killed Mom?

What the fuck?

One text message, and I got it.

Understood why she had the steel around her, why there was barbed wire and No Trespassing signs.

Kill him like you killed Mom.

"Fucking hell," I muttered before crossing over to her.

As I strode through the sand, slipping and sliding because I hadn't bothered to take off my boots, I knew I should pretend I hadn't read the message, pretend we were back in her car and I was coaxing, prodding, poking at her until she stopped icing me out.

Instead, I moved over to her at a rapid clip and blurted with absolutely no finesse, no care, no gentleness, "Why the fuck does your brother think he has the right to text you like this?"

Anabelle had been staring out at the waves, but my question made her spin slowly, jaw falling open.

I opened her purse, yanked out her cell, and shoved it at her.

She took it, eyes dropping to the screen, jaw clenching as she read.

Then she shrugged.

Just shrugged.

And that red on the edges of my vision? It went crimson. "He sent that like it was normal, like it was no big deal." I grabbed her arms, shook her lightly. "Why?" I demanded. "Why the fuck would he say that?"

She went stiff, a fucking statue in my arms.

Then icy words. "Let. Me. Go."

I didn't let her go. Logically, I knew I should have, knew I should have stepped back and given her space. I didn't have the right to demand an explanation. We barely knew each other.

But . . . we weren't strangers.

"Look at that," I said, nodding at a wave crashing along a boulder perched on the sand, its bottom eroded from the constant pounding of the water. "It's inarguably strong, but it's still worn down by the waves, still being reduced, broken down until one day it will be reduced to sand."

Anabelle was quiet, but she'd turned her eyes toward the rock.

Then she sighed. "Are you trying to be a poet?"

I grinned at the tart question, temper fading. "No, Rocky, I'm not."

"Good, because you suck at it."

I was still chuckling when she surprised me by taking my hand and tugging me toward an isolated corner of the beach. "Come on," she said. "I want to show you something."

She stopped in between a pair of rocks, near a visible line between the dry and wet sand where high tide came in but didn't cross.

Shooting me a glare, she tugged the blanket out of my arms, then spread it out before returning for her jacket. "You think you're so handy, don't you? Grabbing all my stuff," she muttered, slipping on her coat and taking her purse. "Don't think I'm going to say thank you. You're the one who all but drove me from the car."

I lifted a brow. "Because I like kissing you?"

"Because you're a stranger who's trying to push your way into my life." A slice of guilt slid through me, but before I could get out an apology, she sat on the blanket, patted the spot next to her, and ordered, "Stop towering over me and sit down already."

Since I wanted to be closer to her, I followed the order.

She sighed when my shoulder brushed hers, then reached

down and slipped off her shoes and socks. I caught a glimpse of gold sparkle polish on her toes before they disappeared beneath the sand, and the idea of this woman covering herself in glitter made me smile. She may want to hide beneath sharp edges, but that wasn't all she was.

I looked forward to uncovering the soft, the sparkle, the light beneath.

"Now yours."

Another order, but another instance where I didn't mind listening to this woman's commands. "Anytime you want me to take off clothing around you, I'm game."

A snort. A roll of her eyes.

"Look," she said after we'd sat there for a moment. "I'm going to level with you. Partly because you're Brooke's brother, but partly because you kiss really well." Humor in those brown eyes, and I couldn't stop myself from stroking her cheek. She nudged me away, not necessarily gently, but also not with any real fire, and I understood why with her next words. "Look, it's nothing to do with you. I don't do relationships. I don't do ties. And I especially do not do them with men like you."

God, this woman was good at pushing people away.

"That's bullshit."

Imperious silence as she turned her head and stared at me, brows raised.

"You made ties with Brooke, with Kace, and Brent, and Iris." I tugged a strand of her hair. "You might like to pretend you're isolated, but you have connections."

She glanced back at the waves. "I didn't do that," she murmured after a long moment. "They . . . pulled me in under their collective wings and just included me to death."

I snorted.

Anabelle turned the full force of her gaze on me. "I'm fucked up, Hayden. I mean it. My head is a mess. My real family can't stand me." A shrug, eyes returning to the ocean. "Until your sister got a hold of me, I didn't have any friends. I'll protect them till my last breath now, and I-I love them. But they don't know all of what is inside me, and if they did . . ."

"They wouldn't want you anymore."

A sigh. "That makes me sound melodramatic, something out of a bad dramatic film, but . . . yeah. I haven't had good results with people liking the person I am inside, so it's not like I'm going to start now."

My heart clenched. "That's sad, Rocky," I said softly.

Narrowed chocolate eyes darting to mine, and I watched as they filled with sparking fury. "You don't know me."

"I know enough to know I want to know you more."

"And that's two fucking *knows* too many."

"I know I like when you snap at me." I tugged another unruly strand of hair, this one being swept up by the wind, being drawn forward over her cheek. Gently, I tucked it back. "And I do know that my sister has good taste in people."

"If by good taste you mean loving a brother who pretends to be dead for years then randomly shows up on Christmas," she muttered.

A bolt of fury darted through me. One, because she was right. Two, because sometimes the truth really fucking stung. "Trying to hurt my feelings?" I asked, deliberately lightening my tone against the guilt that made me want to snap out at her. "Think it'll push me away when it's worked on so many people?"

"No," she said. "I'm just telling the truth. You leaving would just be icing on the cake."

I leaned close. "And what about me kissing you again? More icing? Or more deterrent?"

Her lips parted, and she couldn't hide the shaky exhale, the heat in her eyes.

"No sharp words back?" I cajoled.

"Go fuck yourself."

"Cliché *and* difficult."

"Do you thrive on being an asshole?" she snapped.

"No," I said, cupping her cheek. "I thrive on being with you. I thrive on your scent, your body"—my thumb ran over her bottom lip—"this mouth."

Hot air against my skin, a rapid pulse beneath my fingers.

"I didn't feel anything for close to ten years. Not since I agreed to join an organization for the so-called greater good and left everything that ever meant something to me behind. I didn't feel anything because I couldn't *let* myself, not when I knew that Brooke and Brent were out there hurting. And then when I finally managed to get out, I found that nothing was the same. I can't just be who I was before."

"It's not easy to go back," she murmured.

"That," I said.

Brows pulled together. "What?"

"*That* is why I like you—besides the snark, besides the barbed wire, besides the fact that you're doing your best to push me away. Even putting aside the glorious way you kiss." Her expression didn't relax, and I tapped her nose lightly, smiling at her softly, because this woman was quite simply *more.* "Putting all of that aside, you understand what's in here"—I tapped my temple—"and here"—my chest, just over my heart—"it doesn't make sense, and I don't know *how* I know, but I stare into your eyes and . . . I know you've felt what I've felt."

"That's crazy," she said, but her tone didn't hold any conviction, and I knew she was feeling what I was feeling.

"Doesn't make it any less true."

She sighed.

"Am I right?" I asked, tracing light circles on her jaw.

Another sigh.

"Anabelle?"

That jaw clenched, and fuck if my lips didn't twitch at her stubbornness.

"Rocky."

Eyes on mine, warming from the inside out. "I think the only way we're alike is that we're both stubborn and really fucking like being right."

Since that wasn't untrue, I didn't bother arguing.

Instead, I leaned forward and gave into the temptation of her sexy mouth. But this time instead of letting the instant heat searing through me overwhelm my control, instead of kissing her with all the intensity that was in my gut, my heart, I took it slow, gentle, coaxing.

Like a roly-poly, though I knew she definitely wouldn't like the analogy.

Still, it was apropos. Go too fast and she curled up on herself, covered her soft insides with overlapping armor. Slow and steady and persistent was the only way to move.

"I'm not going to ask you about your family again," I whispered against her lips, trailing my fingers down her arm. "I won't bring up the text messages—"

"You just did," she grumbled, trying to pull back.

I held her tight. "I'm not going to bring it up because there'll be time for that later. Now. Today. I want to know everything else."

So still.

This woman could hold herself absolutely, perfectly still. "It matters though," she said quietly. "What happened."

"I know, baby." I stroked a hand down her hair.

"I didn't," she whispered. "I didn't kill her. I—I—" Her words cut off on a shake of her head.

"I know."

Wide brown eyes. "How?"

I touched the spot above her heart. "Because whatever you're feeling, I'm doing the same."

And more.

I was feeling all that and *more*.

But I didn't say that.

Instead, I slipped an arm around her and cuddled her close, relieved when she let me, relieved enough to ask, "Great, now that that's settled, want to know why I faked my own death?"

ELEVEN

Anabelle

MY BREATH CAUGHT and I chanced looking up at the gorgeous man who should not have a direct line to my heart and yet somehow still did.

"Yes," I said, honestly.

I couldn't lie and say I hadn't thought about doing the same more than a few times when my family surpassed overbearing and held tight to the notion that they should have the right to control everything in my life, from my clothes to my food to my job to my fucking sheets.

Yes, my sister had actually sent me sheets the other week, saying I needed eight-hundred thread-count or I'd get wrinkles.

And a new hairbrush because my hair looked ratty.

But at least that type of motherly intervention—too much and overbearing and had oftentimes felt stifling until I'd moved to Europe, until I'd come back to California when they'd moved to the East Coast—didn't make me feel like shit. Not like my brother, not like the anger that he still held on to, the way he blamed me for my mom dying.

Flat out.

Illogically, I knew.

But the anger was still there, and it still fucking hurt even though I understood logically that I couldn't have been responsible for an illness that had slowly killed my mother by inches.

Not my fault, and yet he still blamed me.

If you didn't keep Mom so busy with your activities, she would

have gone to the doctor sooner.

This was your fault.

Angry words. Untrue words. Illogical words.

Too much so for a successful rocket scientist, one whose strength was thinking linearly. But perhaps it wasn't so strange, not when that strength—grabbing on to an idea then forcefully seeing it through to the end—made him so good at his job.

Yet that same deliberate anger had sliced me to ribbons for far too long.

I was stronger now, could handle it, wouldn't let it break me, and . . . I wasn't feeling that guilt inside because I'd been a difficult pregnancy, a colicky baby, a needy toddler, an overly energetic kid, a demanding teenager.

The baby of the family.

The one my mom had doted over.

The one who'd tried so hard to not disappoint my parents, and couldn't manage it in the end anyway.

Fingers on my cheek, pulling me out of my brain, dropping me back into the present, the sand beneath my feet, the cold whipping my hair around.

"We don't have to talk about anything serious," Hayden murmured, those deep blue eyes on mine. "We can . . . talk about movies."

"Movies?" I asked.

He lay back on the blanket, crossed his arms behind his

head, and I immediately missed his warmth, the gentle way he'd held me. I shouldn't . . . but there were a whole hell of a lot of *shouldn'ts* when it came to this man.

"Yup," he said. "Movies. You're not a rom-com girl, I'm guessing"—he glanced at me and I snorted in answer, making him grin—"action?"

I shook my head.

"Dramas?"

Laughter. "God, no. I've got enough drama in my life."

"Yeah?" he asked. "You gonna tell me about that?"

I sighed, lay down next to him. "How quickly you've changed your tone. First, promising to give me details on your fake death—and don't think I haven't missed the fact you haven't given them yet—then switching your tact to not having to discuss serious stuff, then movies." I rolled to my side, propped my head up on my hand. "Then immediately pumping me for info again. You're a whirlwind, and it's giving me a headache."

"Well, I *have* been dead the last decade," he said, rolling onto his side to face me. "I'm out of practice with the charm offensive."

I chuckled, glared.

He bopped me on the nose.

"I don't want to be amused," I grumbled, "and I definitely don't want to like you."

His smile was a visceral thing, hitting me in the gut, stealing my breath.

"I'm guessing there's a *but* coming." He glanced up at the sky. "But I can't help myself," he said in a poor imitation of my voice. "I now pledge my undying loyalty to you here and now!"

I shook my head, biting my cheek. "You're ridiculous."

A warm chuckle that slid down my spine. "But you're the sexiest man I've ever laid eyes on and now I will prostrate myself at your feet?"

I snorted, amused to my core even though I didn't want to be. Still, I was able to summon at least a *bit* of sass. "Nope," I said, tossing my hair over one shoulder. "No *buts*. It's a simple case of I don't like you."

He grinned. "Liar."

I *was* a liar.

Because I did like him.

And because there had been a *but* coming.

A light tug on a strand of my hair. It should be annoying, that he kept doing that. Instead, I had to fight my smile every time he did it. Hayden amused and teased, and I couldn't remember the last time in my life I had to stop myself from laughing out loud, had to bite my cheek in order to keep my emotions in check.

Nope. It was normally easy for me to be a bitch.

"Hmm." He tugged my hair again. "Then why don't I believe you, Rocky?"

"That's your problem." I huffed out a sigh. "You were going to tell me how you'd faked your death."

"That's true."

I shifted to see him more closely, my tone growing serious. "But Brooke said that you'd told her you couldn't really talk about it."

"I did say that."

I narrowed my eyes. "Well, it's kind of a jerk move to tell me something you wouldn't be willing to tell your sister."

He had a cool sibling.

One who loved him beyond measure, who'd somehow been able to put aside the deception and her need to know every detail.

His eyes went serious. "You're right."

"Or to joke about it. Brooke and Brent were devastated."

"I know," he whispered. "You're right again."

Guilt swept over me and I regretted my words. "No, *I'm* a jerk," I said. "It's not my business, and I'm sure you had your reasons for doing what you did."

"I—"

"Plus, Brooke told me she didn't care about the details as much as she cared about having a second chance with you in her life. As long as you're safe and here, she's happy. That should be the end of my involvement."

"Except she shouldn't be happy," he said, "and I don't want you to not be involved."

"Why not?" I asked, not sure which question I wanted answered.

He made the decision for me. "She shouldn't let me off the hook so easily."

"That we can agree on," I said. "I wouldn't. I'm too good at holding on to grudges."

"Is that something that runs in your family?" he asked.

Ding. Ding. Ding.

"Pushing *again*," I said, but unable to not give a little after he'd just said what he'd said. I added, "But, yes, we Kims are very good at holding on to grudges, really good at internalizing our emotions until they explode into text messages like my brother sent. Thankfully, they're infrequent." I flopped to my back. "Most of the time, my brother is too focused on his work to worry about what the black sheep of the family is doing."

Quiet.

I wrinkled my nose. "I can feel your raised eyebrow from here." Huffing, I shifted to the side, saw I was right. That damn brow was lifted in question. "Just like I can feel you trying to outwait me so that I answer your question. Well, Buster, I'm onto you."

"Buster?" His lips twitched.

Considering I'd never called someone *Buster* in all my life, I figured his smile was warranted. Not that I was going to let him know that. "Yes. I'm onto you. So stop with the secret agent stuff."

"Secret. Agent. Stuff." He chuckled, and I narrowed my eyes. "Sorry," he said, leaning over and slanting his mouth across mine. The kiss was as fast as it was gentle, but my lungs were still sawing when he pulled away and cupped my cheek. "I spent a decade trying to glean every bit of information I could from sources. It's a hazard of the field, but I'll try to be more normal."

"Don't," I blurted.

"Okay." He grinned and I could have kicked myself.

"What kind of information did you glean?" I asked, purposefully changing the subject.

Serious blue eyes. "I can't tell you that."

"Okay." I shivered, though I probably should have been annoyed since he'd gone right back to secret agent stuff, complete with the brooding dark look, with his body coming closer to mine. He was strong. So much stronger than me. And hard. God, I wanted to find out if he was hard everywhere. Swallowing, I grabbed on to my self-control by the barest thread. "Are you using your macho military power to try and get laid?"

"Depends"—a brush of his thumb over my bottom lip—"is it working?"

Heat down my spine, need coalescing in my stomach, moisture gathering between my thighs. Yes, it was. But I wasn't a weakling. I wasn't going to admit to that. "No."

A grin that nearly melted my panties off. "Damn. You're mean, Rocky." A beat. "So, documentaries?"

"What?"

"Your favorite type of movie."

"Oh. No." I paused. "Did you join the secret macho military organization to take down a drug cartel?"

A flash of white, blue eyes dancing. "Nope. Horror?"

"No way." I shuddered. "Was it kids?"

He froze, and I knew with every fiber of my being that Hayden's fake death had to do with kids. With *saving* kids. "I had to do something." He sighed. "The man who had recruited me knew that would be a trigger for me. I don't know if it was my service record—I couldn't help bonding with the kids over there—or just someone had done a workup on my psyche and knew I had a soft spot for them, especially kids caught up in war zones." His jaw clenched.

"They have it so fucking hard, have so little in their lives, and then they can be fucking exploited because some rich person had sick perversions or wanted to make more money off the backs of these kids." He sat up, thrust a hand through his hair. "The guy who brought me in said his team, his agency needed me to help them, that they couldn't save those kids without me." Hayden's jaw clenched. "What he didn't tell me was that *he* was part of it."

I gasped and sat up next to him.

"Yeah," he said, hands clenching into fists on his thighs. "*That.* It took me a while to discover his role and then even longer to clear enough people in the group so that we could shut the ring down. But part of me is still worried that for all the good KTS is doing, it's just as susceptible to the bad guys as the rest of the world."

"KTS?" I asked softly.

His expression clouded. "Fuck, I'm losing my touch."

I bit my lip. "That part was something you shouldn't have shared?"

Regret in those eyes. "Some agent, huh? Can't keep a secret, let alone stop himself from joining a corrupt military organization."

"Is it—" I waffled before deciding to just go for it. "You said there were people you trusted there. People who helped you."

"Yeah. They're cleaning house. Part of me thinks I should have stayed, should have helped and done more. Should have just let everyone continue thinking I was dead instead of coming back and—"

I kissed him this time. "You made a mistake. Let it go. Move on."

Fingers on my cheek, my throat. "I thought you advocated holding grudges."

"Yeah, I do." I covered his hand with mine. He was passionate and haunted and . . . so damned strong. "But you helped people. You followed it through, and now you're searching for something else. You're allowed."

He froze. "That's what Laila said."

"Who's Laila?"

"Someone who had my back."

"Well, you should listen to her," I said. "Sounds like she's smart."

Humor drifting onto his face. "She'd like you." His lips brushed my forehead. "But the truth is I sacrificed my friend and my sister in search of some big ego trip, wanting to be a hero."

"Hayden—"

Another thrust of his hand, mussing those reddish-brown locks. "Brent still won't talk to me."

"Give him time," I said. "He'll come around."

"I fucked up. He told me the recruiter was bad news. I shouldn't have—"

"Did you help the kids?" I asked.

His eyes closed. "Yes," he said. "But there are so many more out there who—"

I covered his hand with mine, not knowing what to say. He was right. *Of course* he was right. The world was filled with plenty of good people, but there would always be those who were willing to hurt others for their own gain. That would never change, no matter how hard this man fought to do the opposite. And that thought gave me the words. "You'll find a way to keep helping."

"I promised Brooke I was out." He shook his head, eyes opening, landing on mine. "I can't keep living a lie."

"So, you help them in another way," I said. "Maybe you don't stay with the group whose name I've already forgotten—" My stomach relaxed when Hayden's mouth curved up. Maybe I wasn't ready to admit to myself or him that I was drawn to him, that I liked him, but the truth was there deep inside. I could keep my distance from the rest of the world.

Hayden was different.

I was fighting a losing battle in keeping my distance from him.

"So," I went on. "Maybe you don't work with them, maybe you *stay* out. But . . . also, maybe you can find another way to help."

Fingers on my cheek. "It's that simple, Rocky?"

"Yeah." I shrugged. "It is."

Chuckling, he shook his head. "Why do I think you're right far too often?"

I grinned. "Because that's fact?"

Those fingers trailed down my arm, sending prickles of heat through my skin, making my breath catch until . . .

"Hayden!" I shrieked as he tickled me, unerringly finding the spot just below my ribs, and holding me tight to him so I couldn't escape. "Oh my God! Stop!" I gasped, writhing against him.

We tumbled back onto the blanket, kicking up sand, my hair tangled over my face.

He kissed me. Long and slow and deep, he kissed me until my pulse thundered, until I was mush beneath him. He kissed me until my lungs burned for air, and even then, I didn't want him to stop. He released my mouth, cupped my cheek in his palm, and said, "Thank you."

Then he kissed me again.

We never did get to my favorite movies.

But in the end, we got much more.

TWELVE

Hayden

I WALKED INTO THE BAR, half-expecting Anabelle to have retreated, to be greeted with that icy glare.

We'd pushed through some barriers the previous day.

On both our sides, and I'd expected withdrawal.

Not the warm smile that arrowed heat to my groin and had me remembering the kiss I'd left her with on her porch, the invitation she'd given, but that I'd turned down. I liked her, knew she was worthy of time to build trust between us.

She deserved to have romance.

And . . . I wanted her to understand with crystal clarity that I wanted her. *Only* her.

"Hey, Rocky," I said, striding over to the bar and reaching over the battered wooden surface to tuck a strand of hair behind her ear. I resisted the urge to twine the silken thread around my finger, but not the one to lean over and press my lips to hers.

She shuddered out a breath when I released her mouth. "Hey . . . *Hay.*"

A twitch of that glorious mouth at her joke.

I ran my thumb over her bottom lip, damp and slightly swollen from my kiss. "You act as though I haven't heard that before."

"New to me." She nudged me back. "Go pester your sister. I'm working here."

Grinning, I leaned back and made my way over to Brooke.

Who was staring at me with raised brows and a shit-eating expression. "How was shopping?"

"Shuddup you," I said, grabbing her in a headlock and giving her a noogie. "You hit your word count?" I asked after I'd released her.

I'd come in late, wanting to catch Anabelle at the end of her shift, but I didn't miss the fact that Brooke's laptop was stowed away, that she was sipping from a glass with a thin red straw, that her face was happy and relaxed.

"Yup. Thank God this book isn't being difficult."

"You say that *now*," Kace said, coming up behind her and pressing a kiss to the top of her head. "But sooner or later your characters are going to start misbehaving."

"Not these ones," Brooke said. "They're perfect angels."

Kace's eyes went hot and I averted my gaze, so I didn't murder the man who dared lay hands on my sister. First, because I knew my sister was a strong woman who could fight her own battles. Second, because I knew Kace was a good man who loved her. And third—my gaze flicked over to Anabelle's and I knew it went hot—I was fully aware that to deny my sister what I was feeling was not only wrong but hypocritical.

However, she was still my sister.

The need to dismember and de-bowel was legit.

Thankfully, I knew better than to do anything to express the turmoil inside on the out—

"Kills you, doesn't it?" Brooke asked.

I blinked, realized I'd been staring at Anabelle, even as she turned away, watching her move efficiently as she managed multiple orders at once.

"Kills me to do what?"

"That I'm all grown up."

I sighed, admitted the truth. "Yeah, Brookie, it does." I sank onto the stool next to her. "I missed a lot. Not just with everything that happened in your life during the last few years, but before that. All the time I was gone. We were barely grown when Mom and Dad died, and I left on my first deployment when you were just leaving for school. Then I came back and—" I shook my head. "I should have—"

"I was okay," she interrupted. "I loved you and we were both doing the best we could with the cards that were dealt to us." She reached over, squeezed my hand. "I stopped looking back the moment I met Kace, because I know that I have so much to look forward to." Her expression took on a dreamy tinge. "Did you know I used to write my books because I never thought there were happy endings for people like you or me? That they were just made up and only found in fiction?" She smiled at Kace. "Then I found someone who was the other half of my heart."

Kace was mixing a drink but must have felt Brooke's gaze on him because he glanced up and . . . he softened.

That was the only way I could think to describe it.

The big, tattooed, often scowling bartender went absolutely soft.

My stare drifted to Anabelle, and though what I had with her was just in its infancy, in the earliest of building stage, I knew in my bones that I—that *we* could be like that, too.

And I wanted it. So fucking bad that I could taste it.

Brooke sighed, and I glanced back toward her, saw she was still staring goo-goo eyes at Kace. But I couldn't tease her. I didn't even want to. Not when she was happy.

"I'm glad, Brookie," I said, nudging her shoulder.

She nudged me back. "So, how are you going to convince Anabelle that she's yours?" She took a sip of her drink. "She's a tough nut to crack."

"Funny story," I said. "But I've got a plan."

"Does your plan involve more shopping?"

I snorted then told the truth. "My plan involves making her fall for me as strongly as I've already fallen for her."

Brooke's brows lifted in surprise. "It's like that?"

"You're the one who insinuated that she might be the other half of my heart, Brookie."

"I know," she whispered. "I mean, I hoped. But really?"

I nodded. "I've never met anyone like her. She's so fucking strong and beautiful and smart." She was also hurt deep inside. But so was I—cut to my core by what I'd seen, what I'd done. And I knew that was part of what had allowed my initial attraction to grow into something more. She felt deeply. She knew pain. But she put her head down and got through. She'd made a life, a family, a place for herself. How could I do anything but fall for her? "I was gone for her the moment she told me off the first time."

Brooke smiled. "Oh, we McAlisters. We never do things the easy way, do we?"

"No, I can't say we do."

"Fall fast, fall deep," she murmured. "Just like Mom and Dad."

I remembered that story, my parents seeing each other at a summer fair of all places, each in line at the cotton candy stand. Their eyes had locked . . . and that was it.

I made a face. "I always hated that story," I told her. "Could never believe it was true. It just sounded . . ."

Fake. Ridiculous. Fairytale.

"I loved it," Brooke said. She sighed. "I used to go to the fair and hope that I would meet my soulmate." She wrinkled her nose. "Unfortunately, the only person who tried to pick me up was Mikey Harrison, and that was after I ate a jumbo corn dog."

I shuddered. "No more talk of jumbo corn dogs."

A wicked grin as she picked up her glass, started to sip. "Oh, does your plan not involve *your* jumbo—"

I tipped up the bottom of her drink.

She gasped and almost spilled it on herself, shooting me a dark glare. "This is my celebratory word count drink, and you almost made me drop it."

"I love you, Brookie."

Her eyes widened, and maybe they went a little damp, but I wasn't able to totally discern that because she set down her glass and threw her arms around my neck, hugging me tight. "I love you, too, Hayden. I'm so glad you're back."

I squeezed her back, another apology on the tip of my tongue, but before I could get it out, she dropped her arms and glared. "None of that."

"Brookie," I began.

"Forward," she said. "We look forward now."

I sucked in a breath, released it slowly. "Okay."

"Good." She waved at Kace. "Now, let's get you a drink, and you can tell me all about your plan and how it involves corn dogs."

Of course, Kace chose that moment to appear in front of us.

He stopped, brows raised. "Do I want to know?"

Brooke smiled wide. "Do you like corn dogs?"

I sighed, shook my head. "Enough with the corn dogs already. I'll tell you everything you want to know."

"Muah-ha-ha," she said, rubbing her hands together. "And so my evil plan has worked."

"I'll just grab you a beer," Kace said as he backed away slowly.

I couldn't blame the man.

My sister was ridiculous and awesome and—

"I love you," I told her again.

"Yeah, yeah, you said that already." She waved a hand. "Just because you were dead for ten years doesn't mean you have to tell me every second."

I grinned. "Did you learn that snark from Anabelle?"

A nod, a dainty sip of her drink. "I learned that snark on my own, thank you very much."

Kace dropped a beer in front of me. "And from Anabelle."

I snorted.

Brooke huffed.

Kace turned to me, eyes dancing with amusement. "So, now, what's this about corn dogs?"

My sister snickered. I shook my head in disgust.

And then because I was with my family, because I was home, because I was finally starting to look forward with my life instead of toward the past, I told them my plan.

When I finished, Brooke leaned back on her stool, lips curved in satisfaction. "That's *so* much better than corn dogs."

———

This time I knocked.

Instead of spending an hour in my car. Instead, of waffling for twenty minutes on the porch, I knocked.

Mostly, that was because Brooke was next to me.

She was meeting Brent for coffee. I was hijacking their hangout.

The door opened. "Hey, Broo—" His eyes narrowed when they landed on me. "Sorry, I can't meet today. Too much homework."

Brooke sighed, stuck her hand out when he started to

retreat. "Nice try. You already told me that you had a test yesterday and had today off." She wove her other arm through Brent's. "Come on, Iris is waiting for us and promised me apple turnovers."

Brent didn't move.

She tugged.

Brent sighed and shut the door behind him then let Brooke lead him down the sidewalk. The man could hold a grudge, had always been able to. He'd once not talked to me for three weeks after we'd returned stateside because I'd accidentally knocked over his beer.

Which, I got, because beer was in short supply and there was nothing better than the first one hitting your lips when returning home.

But three weeks for a beer.

Fuck, how long would it be for a fake death?

An eternity.

Stifling a sigh, I followed them down the driveway and in the direction of Iris's place of business—more information garnered from my keeping tabs from the wrong side of the grave. She had a small industrial kitchen not far from her house, a house Brent had moved into when things got serious.

Brooke glanced over her shoulder at me, tilted her head. "Oh, that's my phone." She let go of Brent's arm, slowed her pace as she lifted it to her ear. "Kace? Hi, baby."

I took her spot, not exactly smooth, but definitely determined. "I'm sorry, I hurt you," I said without preamble, knowing that I needed to own up and just level with him. "I'm going to do my best to make it up to you and Brooke."

Brent didn't acknowledge me, just kept walking.

Trying again, I said, "I heard you went back to school."

A shrug.

"What are you studying?"

A grunt.

"Caveman?" I asked, unable to hold back the snark. Maybe Anabelle was rubbing off on me too. "Wow. I'm impressed."

A roll of his eyes, but he sighed and said, "Economics."

"Whoa."

"What? You think I can't?"

"Fuck, no," I said, honestly. "You're one of the smartest people I know. I think that's awesome. I'm just a dumbass with a gun, who can occasionally make something happen with computers."

Another grunt.

"What can you do with an econ degree? Financial planning?"

"Yeah," he said. "But I'm thinking corporate accounting. I've been doing some interesting projects with—"

He seemed to catch himself, to realize he was talking to me, and frowned.

"Anyway, should be good."

A moment of unfreezing, then back to the grudge.

I reminded myself to be patient. I had trust I needed to rebuild with him, and that would take time. "How close are you to finishing—"

"Stop pretending to make kissy noises to Kace back there, darlin'," Brent called. "You're not that good of an actor."

"Hmph," she said, but didn't deny that she'd been faking. Instead, she laced both of her arms through one of ours and started walking again, leading us toward Iris's kitchen.

"You two need to kiss and make up," she ordered. "You know you want to."

I did. Well, not the kissing part as much as I wanted my friend back.

But Brent was firmly in grudge state and as thus, didn't

acknowledge Brooke's words. Instead, he began talking about how Iris wanted to get married near Christmas next year.

"Oh!" Brooke said, getting distracted from her quest for my forgiveness and totally consumed by the details of a Christmas wedding. "If Kace ever gets his ass in gear and proposes, we could have a joint wedding! That would be so cool! Red and gold as the colors. Twinkly lights and glitter everywhere. *All* the Christmas trees . . ."

Distracted thoroughly. As Brent had intended, I knew.

"We could even have one of those muff thingies to keep our hands warm . . ."

I met his eyes for a split second before he deliberately looked away and nodded at Brooke. "Sure. If Iris wants it."

"It's going to be so cool!"

I smiled at Brooke's enthusiasm, even as I knew that at this point, my invite to the wedding was about as likely as Brent suddenly deciding to take up tap-dancing.

That being infinitesimally small.

But I would like to see him get married.

Maybe as much as I'd like to see the tap routine.

Smiling to myself, I pushed down my impatience, knowing not everything could be smoothed over as easily as it had with Brooke. The way to move forward was paved with patience, slow and steady steps and persistence.

Lots and lots of persistence.

Luckily, I had that in spades.

THIRTEEN

Anabelle

I'D BEEN HAD.

I pulled the front door to the cottage closed behind me, making sure the latch caught and stared down at the brown paper bag on the porch in front of me.

The reason I'd been had.

Molly's Bakery

An insulated cup sat next to it, and I could smell the freshly ground coffee in the air.

Narrowing my eyes, I glanced around, trying to find the person—read: the man—who'd left me the treats. But the space around me was quiet, nothing but the quiet shush of the wind blowing through the trees.

He had been there, though.

And he'd brought the big guns.

"Are you going to keep staring at it like it's a snake?" Hayden's deep voice slid over my body like a second skin, raising goose bumps, wrapping me in warmth. That caused an immediate blip of panic to follow in its wake, but that alarm wasn't enough to pull me back.

Frankly, I wanted this man too much, and it overrode any of my usual attempts at keeping my distance and self-preservation.

"Is it poisoned?" I asked.

He grinned, climbing up the stairs and bending to snag the cup and bag. One sip out of the coffee—trailed by an "Ah!"— before he stopped in front of me. "Not poisoned."

I narrowed my eyes, breath catching at the beauty of him. It was early morning—for me, that was—just after ten and the sunlight gilded his skin, brought out the streaks of red and gold hidden in the brown of his hair, made the blue of his eyes beyond bright.

He was gorgeous.

But he was also nice and funny and pushy and . . . I liked him.

"What are you doing here?" I asked.

"I wanted to see you."

See? He just came out and said things like that, making him impossible to resist, impossible to dislike.

It scared me.

Made me retreat, made me lash out.

Don't let him get too close. Don't open that side of myself again. I'd closed it down after losing my mom, after my brother's anger, after my dad's disappointment, and I couldn't risk opening it again.

"Well, I'm tired," I said, spinning and reaching for the door handle, my heart in my throat.

"Hi, Tired."

I frowned, froze with my fingers on the handle. "What?"

"You said you're tired . . ." A beat. "So, hi, Tired."

"That's the worst joke I've ever heard." I turned, saw he was leaning back against a pillar.

And proving once again that he had easy humor, he merely laughed. "Yup. Right up there in the realm of Dad Jokes." Then he continued with the proving, or maybe it was that he continued reinforcing his ability to give, because then he said, "That used to be my dad's favorite joke." Quiet words, sad eyes. "We'd say *I'm bored* or *I'm tired* or *I'm mad* and he'd say, *Hi, Bored* or *Tired* or *Mad.*"

My lips twitched. "So, you're saying bad jokes run in the family?"

"Yup." A nod. "Ingrained in my DNA." He cocked his head. "What's in yours?"

"Book smarts, an ability to hold grudges, and keeping our emotions under wraps until one of us sends a text message or makes a phone call that eviscerates the other person."

Blue eyes went wide, but that was the only part of Hayden that moved.

I, on the other hand, had to lock every muscle in my body in order to not clamp a palm over my mouth to stop any further verbal vomiting.

I'd revealed too much.

Too fucking much.

"Breathe," Hayden said.

Air shuddered out of my lungs even before I realized I'd been holding my breath.

"That's better," he murmured and sank down onto the top step. The crinkle of the bag opening drew my focus, pulled me out of the words that had been circling in my head since the beach.

"It's never been that bad before," I whispered.

"The messages?"

I nodded.

He patted the spot next to him, and I crossed the porch, sat down on that top step, just a few inches separating us.

"Here." He handed me the cup. "Have you ever thought to just tell them that it hurts you this bad?"

I wrapped my fingers around the coffee. "I don't think my brother would care. He's looking for someone to blame, and I'm a convenient target."

"Why?"

"Why what?" I asked.

"Why are you letting yourself be a target?" he asked. "Why take the abuse?"

"I—"

I stopped, lungs freezing, but he didn't press me for an answer, just let me get my thoughts in order, gave me time to realize that for as strong as I liked to think I was, I had just let my family walk all over me.

Because, deep down, there was a piece of me that thought I deserved it.

Fuck.

"I never thought of it that way," I whispered. "I just . . . always accepted that it was the way it was, that I owned that burden because—" My words cut off, the painful truth too much to accept.

"It's not your fault," he said, shifting so his shoulder rested against mine. "But logical and rational thought doesn't always rule when it comes to families."

"No," I said. "It doesn't."

"You know the best thing about learning something about yourself?"

A shake of my head. "No."

"When you learn it, you get to put it to use."

"AKA not let my family walk over me?"

"Ding. Ding. Ding." He tapped my nose, affecting a game show announcer's voice. "The prize goes to . . . Anabelle Kim."

"Idiot," I said with a snort. "Why didn't you just knock and wait for me to come to the door?" I asked, sipping and nearly moaning. Iris was a superb baker, but she didn't do coffee like *Molly's*.

"Would you have answered?"

No.

Maybe?

"That's a no." Hayden laughed and pulled out a pumpkin muffin from the bag—my favorite, damn him and his sources— handing it over to me with a smile.

I sighed and took it.

Maybe he was being pushy, but there was no way I was turning down baked goods.

He was tempting beyond measure, but for as cavalier as I'd pretended to be about Tom's text, I was hurt. He'd said some stuff after Mom died, some bad stuff, but I'd been able to compartmentalize it away, chalk it up to grief.

Over the years, he'd been judgy, snarky, sometimes cold, but not angry, not like that. And the sudden resurgence made my nerves twist themselves into knots.

I wanted to hide and mope and figure out what was going on.

Plus, my landlords had left me a message saying they'd received an offer on the house before they'd even put it on the market. If the inspection went through, the property was going to be in new hands.

So . . . that was going to be interesting.

"Your brother hurt you," he whispered when I'd just nibbled off a corner of the muffin before resting it and the hand holding it on my leg.

"Yeah," I said. "Stupid, huh?"

"No, Rocky." Fingers on my cheek, my jaw, my hair. "Not stupid. Just because you have the logic and the plan to move forward doesn't mean all of the hurt just disappears."

"I don't understand," I admitted. "That's what makes it worse, I think. We used to have fun together, be able to talk about so many different things, but since my mom passed, every conversation is a minefield. And the messages . . . it's like the moment he remembers she died, all of the hate bubbles up. It doesn't help that my dad blames me for her death, too. At least in part."

"That's—"

"Probably true," I interrupted. "At least in some way. My pregnancy was difficult for her to recover from, and I took a lot of physical and emotional energy growing up." My eyes flicked up to his. "Did I give her cancer?" I shook my head. "Of course not. But do I feel like if I'd been a little easier, less demanding on her time that she would have gone to the doctor sooner?" A shrug. "Maybe."

"I'm not going to say that's being unfair to yourself," he murmured. "It's hard to separate those feelings of guilt when you lose people you care about."

"Why do I feel like there's a but coming?" I asked, stealing some of his words.

He grinned. "Because there is."

"Of course."

A serious expression transformed his face from amused to stern. "*But* you have to stop punishing yourself for things you can't control. You did the best you could. You loved her, and you love *them*, otherwise the words wouldn't hurt so much."

I made a face.

He tugged a strand of my hair. "It's not easy."

"Yeah." I sighed, a rueful smile on my lips. "It's not."

"In the meantime"—he nudged my hand, lifting it, and the muffin in its grasp, back up to my mouth—"should we drown our sorrows with carbs?"

My lips twitched. "And what sorrows are you drowning in?"

Hayden gave me a morose look. "The ones where the beautiful woman I'm crazy about refuses to invite me into her house."

Laughing, I took a bite of the muffin, nearly moaned at its deliciousness. "I invited you in last time you were here, if you recall."

"Hmm." He tapped his chin. "Don't recall that."

I snorted. "Then you'd better be happy with the fact that she allowed you onto the front porch." I mock-glared. "Consider that a victory."

Steady blue eyes on mine. "I do, Rocky."

Breathing not quite steady, I kept eating the muffin, staring out at the backyard, at the trees, at the partly cloudy sky until I'd steadied myself, until I could look at Hayden and say the thing that had been bothering me. "You could have any girl. Not some frumpy—"

Lips on mine, fingers in my hair, the remains of the muffin falling to the ground as he stole my mouth in a hot kiss that made my head spin, made my pulse that had just found steady ground skitter and jump, my lungs burn with the need to draw in air.

Only then did he pull away.

Not far, and for the first time I could admit without fear that I hadn't wanted him to take his mouth from mine, that I could have continued kissing Hayden for eternity.

"I don't want anyone else," he said, lightly tracing his finger down my nose. "I just want you."

Words. Just words.

But also words that gave a girl like me hope.

Words that wove their way through the cracks in the walls surrounding my heart, began forming roots, burrowing in until I knew there would be no way to excise them.

A blip of fear.

But before it could fully coalesce and take over, Hayden tapped my cheek lightly and asked, "Appletini?"

Fear forgotten, I burst out laughing. "No, McAlister. I don't think you're putting your secret agent skills to proper use."

"Hmm." Another long, drugging kiss. "I'll do better."

He wasn't lying.

Because he did do better. So much better that those roots grew into seedlings, into a healthy plant, into hope that my life could be more than I'd ever expected.

FOURTEEN

Hayden

OPERATION WIN ROCKY Over was off to a good start.

We'd hung on her front porch for just over an hour, me confessing that I had, in fact, been putting my "secret agent skills" to use by tracking down some of her favorite things.

I didn't tell her it had been easy, that because her friends wanted her to be happy, they'd dished up facts readily.

Brooke wanted us both happy, and she'd given up the goods on all things Anabelle preferred then had sent me to Iris for additional information the next morning for further intel. Thankfully, Iris felt the same way, or at least that she wanted Anabelle to find someone who cared for her as much as Anabelle cared for the people in her circle.

"She deserves to have someone want to learn all the little details about her," Iris had said when I'd shown up at her bakery early that morning, wondering how I'd win her over in order to get more dirt and then purchase some baked goods to ply Anabelle with.

"I agree," I had said. Simple truth.

Her eyes, a startling blue-green, had fixed me in place for long moments. "If you're going to be with her, you need to be that guy."

"I intend to be," I told her.

We'd stood there in silence for several minutes as she'd continued to take my measure. Finally, she sighed and nodded, her face gentling. "I think you can be." She touched my arm, sighed again. "Brent misses you."

"I miss him as well," I said. "And I'm working on that, too."

"He's stubborn," she murmured.

"Yup."

Lips curving. "Let it be known, he's got a soft spot for cherry pie."

"Tequila, cherry pie, and cute little blondes who are obsessed with Christmas nutcrackers," I teased. "Don't think I didn't see your very large collection. You trying to torment my friend?"

She snorted and smacked me lightly, before returning to kneading a large pile of dough in front of her. "Okay, maybe a little." A sly smile, finger and thumb held up, mere centimeters apart.

"About that cherry pie," I began, "happen to know where I can find some?"

A finger tapping her lips. "Hmm. Maybe?" Then she'd patted my cheek, surprised me with a hug and said, "Come to dinner Saturday night. We'll work on Brent." A beat. "I promise I'll lock up the nutcrackers."

I'd laughed, but my throat had gone tight from her teasing, from her help and acceptance. Brookie had done so good to surround herself with these folks.

"Don't be sad," Iris murmured. "It'll all work out."

"Yeah?"

A nod. "Yeah."

"Thank you."

Iris had just given me another squeeze, and I could have sworn that there was a trace of mischief in her eyes when she stepped back and told me, "Bring a bottle of whiskey. Single malt."

But by the time I'd caught it, the trace was gone, her eyes on the counter in front of her and the intricate braid of dough she had laid out on the steel.

We'd chatted a few minutes, the soft-spoken baker's eyes narrowing dangerously when she told me that Anabelle liked the pumpkin muffins at a place in San Francisco called *Molly's* better than Iris's own.

"I'll defeat my enemy on the baking battlefield," she'd growled, although the effect had been slightly diminished by the fact that she had a streak of flour on her cheek.

"Of that, I have no doubt."

She slapped another pile of dough down, began kneading. "And then I will be victorious!" Grinning at me, she'd given the directions to *Molly's* then shooed me out of the kitchen, so I had time to make the drive and get back to Anabelle's place.

Pumpkin muffins and an Americano.

Not bad for an opening shot.

But today, I had another plan.

I was behind the large tree in Anabelle's backyard, watching and waiting after having just deposited another bag on her porch.

Not food this time, but something I'd had the merest glimpse of in the form of a tattoo on her wrist, something I'd confirmed from Brooke's list of all things Anabelle.

The doorknob rattled, and I shifted farther into the shadows, wanting to see if her reaction was going to be all I hoped. The wooden panel slid open, shapely jean-clad legs emerged, and I took my time allowing my gaze to drift from her calves up to her sexy hips, to the pale blue sweater draped over her frame. It hinted at curves beneath, made my fingers tingle with the urge to touch.

But I forced myself to keep looking up, to take in her expression as she halted—eyes wide, lips parted, the palest pink appearing on her cheeks.

Then she smiled.

And, just like that, I tumbled headfirst into love. I'd pretty much been there, whether it was McAlister genes or just the onslaught of this woman. But in my head, there was no more equivocating or saying it was too soon. This woman was it for me.

Porches.

My kryptonite.

Well, if they kept bringing me this woman, then I wasn't going to complain.

She bent and picked up the bag, taking it to the top step and sitting down with it in her lap.

Then she peeled open the flap and . . . burst out laughing.

Exactly the reaction I'd been hoping for.

Anabelle reached into the bag, pulled out the coasters I'd found that had sayings from one of her favorite shows—not that *she'd* told me that, since I still hadn't even pinned her down on movies or cocktails yet. I had forbidden Brooke and Iris from telling me, knowing there were some things I needed to discover for myself.

The TV show info I'd taken.

And I'd been glad I'd done so when I'd seen the shop in San Francisco the previous day, merch from her favorite reality show on full display.

Now, she had a set of coasters for her favorite drink that I still didn't know.

Her gaze lifted after she'd gone through the five wooden squares. "Come on out, secret agent man. I want to kiss you properly."

Seeing as I wanted that, too, I stepped out from behind the tree.

Anabelle shook her head, lips still curved. "Okay, I can admit you still have some skills, given the way you just materialized out of shadows."

Chuckling, I made my way over to her. "You didn't look below," I said.

Because while her tattoo didn't relate to the show, it *did* relate to something else I'd seen in those San Franciscan shops.

"What?" she asked, brows drawn together.

I snagged the bag, pulled out the tissue paper, and handed her the tiny box inside.

"Hayden," she began.

"Open it."

She tugged off the lid and froze, every single muscle in her body going stiff for long moments, long enough that I felt a trickle of fear in thinking that I'd done the wrong thing.

But then she carefully tugged one of the earrings free. They were shaped like tiny hermit crabs, the pattern nearly identical to the small tattoo on her wrist.

"I—" Her eyes found mine. "How?"

I brushed my fingers over her wrist. "I pay attention."

She threw her arms around my neck, hauled me close, and gave me a kiss that sent my pulse skyrocketing, my cock hardening to granite. Her tongue brushed mine, her hands wove into my hair, the earring the smallest pinprick of pain.

Because she was close.

Because her mouth was on mine, her body was pressed to mine.

Because her heart was slowly becoming mine.

Measured and steady and persistent. I was going to win this girl.

FIFTEEN

Anabelle

I WATCHED Hayden's back as he left, having turned down my invitation inside because he had a meeting for the house he was going to purchase.

Apparently, everything had gone through as it should, and he'd have occupancy to his new place in two weeks.

Two weeks he'd told me, after I'd managed to stop kissing the man for being sweet and thoughtful—*and* pushy—that couldn't come soon enough. Apparently, living with newlyweds wasn't ideal, least of all when one of those newlyweds was his sister.

Either way, I could fully admit, without panic, thank me very much, that I liked the idea of him staying nearby.

He was . . . special.

And I . . . well, I really liked him. Maybe more than liked him, but that was a trail I couldn't allow myself to go down, not if I liked the whole not panicking thing.

Regardless, I was happy he was staying.

Especially if he kept showing up on my porch.

Hay stopped at the corner of the fence, glanced back, and smiled. But damn, did the man have a sexy smile.

I lifted my hand in a wave. He waved back.

Then he was gone, slipping through the gate and disappearing out into the street.

Disappointment. Yup, it was real.

I glanced down at the box holding the hermit crab earrings. I'd explained to him what they meant as we'd sat on the porch, but I still couldn't believe he'd noticed the tiny tattoo on the inside of my wrist, even with the long sleeves.

I'd gotten the ink for my mom.

She'd had a pet hermit crab named Ted for years when we were growing up, would always spend too much time decorating different shells for him to try on. Sparkles and rhinestones, fancy beads, all attached with superglue. That crab had more bling than most celebrities, and that didn't even include the hours she'd spent drawing different "crabby" designs in fine point markers.

Ted had enjoyed a charmed lifestyle, with fresh food and water, those shells, and a palatial enclosure.

He'd died just a few weeks before my mom, as though part of him had known the end was coming.

Great. Now I was anthropomorphizing a crab.

Still, I couldn't deny they'd had a connection. I'd seen him crawl far too often over my mom, perching on her hand, slowly making his way up to her shoulder and hiding in her hair.

Ah, Ted. She'd loved him, and I'd put him on my arm. After far too many drinks one night in Berlin, in a sketchy looking tattoo studio, all while blabbering to the artist about sparkly seashells.

It was a miracle it had turned out as great as it had.

I ran a finger over the silver charm. And now I had another

memory to add to the box I had tucked deep inside my heart. My mom. Ted. Hayden and his thoughtfulness.

Sighing, in happiness rather than impatience for once, I headed into the house.

Enough mooning over Hayden.

I had errands to run, groceries to buy, laundry to do, and . . . I grinned because I had one other stop to make before I went into work that night. I had no doubt that Hayden would show up, but this time I wouldn't be empty-handed.

He'd been paying attention. Well, so had I. He'd been slowly winning me over. I wasn't going to be the only one falling. He'd pushed, and I was going to push right back.

Nodding to myself, I headed into my bedroom, setting the box on my dresser, taking a moment to run my finger over the tiny claw on the earring, not needing to make the decision, not when it had already been made. I couldn't pinpoint exactly when it had happened, but I thought it correlated with pumpkin muffins, or maybe it was warm sand beneath my toes, or maybe it was porches.

"Doesn't matter," I whispered, using the mirror to slip the earrings on and feeling closer to my mom . . . to myself . . . to another person than I'd felt in so many years.

Accepting the choice was almost easy, as though Hayden had the key to unlock my shields. Or maybe it was effortless because he'd opened his wide.

Regardless, the decision to stop hiding and to explore whatever it was between me and Hayden was similar to the one that had kept me in Europe, instead of the one that had made me go in the first place.

I was going to live rather than run.

And the first thing I did in the living category was text my brother back, instead of ignoring the messages like I normally would have, instead of just bearing the brunt of his anger and trying to dutifully move forward.

I wasn't doing that anymore.

I was standing up for myself. I was done with shouldering more guilt and blame and self-recrimination.

It was just . . . enough.

My fingers flew across the keyboard, typing the words fast and furious, and before I could second-guess myself, I hit the button to send the message.

I didn't kill her, and you're an asshole for saying that.

Maybe not the nicest or most mature words, or even the most eloquent.

But it was a start.

And as Hayden had pointed out, sometimes knowing that something had to be done or wasn't right, didn't always translate to feeling whole and healed. I needed to be patient and take those baby steps and keep moving forward.

A month ago, I wouldn't have been able to get there.

With him in my life, I knew that it was an inevitability.

———

LAST CALL HAD COME and gone.

Hayden hadn't shown.

I had a box burning a hole in the bottom of my purse, and the man hadn't come.

"Fucker," I muttered, stacking the last glass in the tray, knowing I was being unreasonable. He hadn't actually said he was going to come into the bar that night, and it was Kace's day off. He and Brooke and Hayden were probably doing family things.

The glasses rattled as I shoved them into the dishwasher.

It was the final tray. The bar was empty, its front door locked, the alarm set behind Brent as I'd shooed him out the door to get home to Iris.

At least they'd invited me to dinner on Saturday. I'd get yummy baked goods and get to hang out with my friends before heading into the bar to work my closing shift.

We used to alternate the big nights—Friday and Saturday—but Brent had asked for them off not long after things had gotten serious with him and Iris. Not that he wasn't willing to fill in, but he preferred to have his off days line up with Iris's, and since he'd gone back to school and his degree was nearly complete, I knew that his nights of working closing shifts alongside me were numbered.

He'd switch to swing, or to days, and then when he moved on from bartending, I wouldn't see him as often.

Sighing, I glanced around the bar that had become home in so many ways and couldn't stop the pulse of sad from creeping through me. But that sad was tempered. Brent would soon have a career that brought him bigger and better things . . . and a schedule that aligned more closely with Iris's early mornings.

Brent wasn't a lifer. Had never been.

And what was I?

That I wasn't sure of yet. Not an academic. Not an East Coast, familial black sheep who moved in with her sister and father.

Just a bartender.

For now, that was enough.

Kace was different. He had a clear path. He was the owner, enjoyed being behind the bar, though on quiet weeknights, disappeared into the office to do owner things.

Snorting, I perused the space behind the bar, made sure we were set for the next day, before pulling the tray of glasses out of the dishwasher when it dinged. One final walk into the front room, a glance to confirm the door was locked, the space empty, before I headed to the office to grab my backpack.

Heavier because of the box inside. A box that Hayden hadn't shown up to receive. *Ugh.*

I made a face before turning off the alarm so I could leave without triggering it. Then I punched in the code on the panel to start the countdown timer for a second time, walked down the hall, and pushed open the door.

"Hey, Rocky."

I nearly screamed as I all but jumped out of my skin.

Hayden was there, in the shadows.

I clasped a hand to my chest, glared over at him. "What the fuck is wrong with you?"

A flash of white in the dark of night, the tall, beautiful, wonderful man I'd just started to call my own coming to my side, tugging lightly on a strand my hair before tucking it behind my ear. "You locked me out," he said with all the charm of a schoolboy, leaning close enough that I could feel the heat of his breath on my skin.

"Well, *you* missed last call," I said tartly, pushing past him and heading to my car, even though I wanted to lean closer, wanted to turn my head and press my lips to his. "If you'd come before we closed, you wouldn't have gotten locked out."

He began walking beside me. "I was busy."

I sniffed, kept moving to my car.

"Itching for a fight, Rocky?"

"No." Though, I supposed I was. I had been waiting for him all night, the need to see him a perpetual prickle under my skin.

Hot breath on my ear. "Liar."

I reached into my backpack to extract my keys, but instead my fingers grasped the box, tugged it out. "Here," I grumbled, slapping it against his chest.

"What's this?" he asked, taking it.

"Nothing," I muttered, grabbing my keys next and unlocking my door. "Did you drive?"

He was staring down at the present, wrapped in Christmas paper since I'd had some left, and it fit . . . and also because I wasn't the type of woman to have wrapping paper of various kinds at my place. More power to those peeps who did, but I usually defaulted to gift cards, and if I did have an idea for a present for my friends or family, then I defaulted to a gift bag and tissue paper.

Sometimes it matched.

Sometimes it didn't.

I could never get the floof of paper coming out of the top of the bag right.

But it wrapped the gift, and it was what was inside that was more important anyway, right?

Right.

Inner monologue about wrapping paper choices aside, I realized Hayden hadn't moved, was frozen, holding the box to his chest.

"Hay?" I asked.

He blinked. "Yeah, Rocky?"

"Did you drive?"

His eyes met mine, and I was confused by the slight haze in them. As though he were shocked that I might have bought him something, even after he'd been peppering me with treats. Not to mention, Brooke was generous with her affection. I couldn't imagine she wouldn't have bought him presents.

Or maybe it wasn't that?

"No," he said, shaking his head, that haze disappearing. "I didn't drive." One half of his mouth curved up. "I thought I'd bum a ride."

I sighed, pretending to be put out, but instead I grabbed the handle to the driver's door, inclined my head to the other side, and said, "Get in."

"Bossy."

"You like it," I said, starting to sit in the driver's seat when his voice drifted to my ears.

"Yeah, I do."

I grinned, tossed my knapsack in the back, dropped the rest of the way into my seat, locked up, and buckled in before turning on the car. "You going to open that?"

"You going to tell me what's inside?"

"Nope." I began backing out of the stall. "You still at Brooke's?" I asked. "Or have you given in and booked yourself a hotel room?"

"Still at Brooke's," he grumbled. "But they're having a date night in." He made a vomiting sound.

"Is this your way of trying to finagle an invitation to my place?"

"Your porch is comfier."

I snorted.

"What's in the box, baby?"

The endearment and the soft tone make my heart skip a beat, filled me with warmth. "Two things." I shrugged, affecting casual as I turned out of the driveway and began driving back to my place. "Well, three."

"Three?"

I glanced over, saw his eyebrows had lifted.

"Yes, three."

"Hmm."

Sighing as I turned onto the street that would lead to my place, I demanded, "What? Are you waiting for an invitation to open it?"

"No," he said. "I was waiting for your porch." A beat. "And for your ass to be on that top step because I know the moment I open this, I'm going to want to kiss that gorgeous mouth, and I'd prefer to do it when you weren't operating a motor vehicle."

"I could pull over," I pointed out.

"Then I couldn't finagle an invitation into your house."

Luckily, he said that at the same moment I'd pulled into the driveway, so I was able to do what I'd been craving since the moment I first saw him outside the bar.

I wrapped my arms around his neck and kissed him.

The box poked me in the chest, the gear shift in my thigh, the console in my stomach.

And I didn't give one fuck.

Because Hayden's mouth, his lips, his tongue and teeth and the way he didn't hesitate to kiss me back, and how one hand gently cupped my cheek all the while . . . that's what I gave fucks about.

So many fucks.

All the fucks.

Now if only I could get him to—

He pulled back, palm on my face, eyes hot. "Why are you smiling?"

"Because I really like kissing you."

I leaned back, knowing that even though I wanted to keep kissing him, I wanted to continue it in a place where I wasn't being jabbed in the thigh, in the stomach, in the chest more.

There were so many other places I'd rather be poked.

Heh.

I popped the handle and got out of the car, quite pleased with myself. At least until after I'd reached back in and grabbed my bag.

Because I might have been on top, having gotten the better of Hayden for a second, but he was a big, super, secret agent who had many skills to put to use. The first of which was snagging my backpack from my hand. The second was plucking my keys from my fingers. The third—

Well, I couldn't complain about the third.

Because the third was him scooping me up, pinning me against the side of my car, and kissing me until I could hardly see straight.

"Legs around my waist, Rocky," he ordered roughly when he released my mouth to trail his lips down my throat.

I had no problem following that particular order.

Especially when it brought my mouth close to his, close enough that I was able to steal his lips for another kiss.

Distantly, I heard the car door slam, the locks bleep as he hit the button on the key fob. But realistically, I didn't hear anything.

Instead, I felt.

His mouth on mine. His strong arms, but his gentle hold. The cool air kissing heated skin. The shifts in my body weight as he carried me up the three steps to the porch. The slow slide as he lowered me down, every inch of my front rubbing against every inch of his until my feet hit the wood.

"I should open this," he murmured, nuzzling at my throat, the cool silk of his hair brushing my skin. "Then let you get some rest."

"Or," I said, "you can open it inside."

SIXTEEN

Hayden

"ROCKY," I began.

She snagged the keys from my hand, unlocked and opened the door. Then strolled inside, leaving it pushed wide.

What was I supposed to do?

I needed to close it.

Which I could do from the porch, but then it wouldn't be locked, and I'd be right back at square one, and *square one* definitely wasn't following the sexiest woman I'd ever laid eyes on into her place, the invitation from her tongue lingering in my ears, but the invitation from those swaying hips even more tempting.

All sleek female curves in one tiny package.

Small enough to pick up and pin against the car, against a wall. Tiny enough that I could kiss her as I carried her. Petite enough—

"You coming?"

Probably best she stopped me before I went any further down that particular thesaurus train of thought.

"No," I said, crossing over the threshold, setting the box on the small table she had just inside the hall. "Not yet anyway." I kicked the door shut, flicked the lock, and closed the distance between us. "But you're about to."

That line should have had me thrown out of the house.

Instead, she giggled and slipped her arms around my waist, rose up on tiptoe, and smirked. "What other bad pickup lines do you have for me?"

I swept her up into my arms. "The question is, what *don't* I have for you." I waggled my brows, loving the little titter from the tough as nails woman in front of me. Loving it so much that my cock, which had basically been steel from the moment her lips had met mine outside the car, hardened further, pressing painfully against my zipper, and I was reminded again how long it had been for me.

And how careful I needed to be so that I didn't embarrass myself, didn't disappoint her.

"Where's your bedroom?" I asked.

"Aren't you going to open your present?"

"I'm going to open something else."

She smiled, rested her head against my collarbone. "Pun-tastic," she murmured, "but . . . I'd really like you to open the present."

The hint of uncertainty in her tone made me freeze then carry her to the couch.

"Okay, Rocky." I set her down, grabbed the box then returned to her side, sitting next to her and tearing open the Christmas paper. Inside was—

Fuck.

My heart squeezed hard when I saw the first item, instantly recognizing it as a welcome mat.

Carefully, I unrolled it and snorted out a laugh when I saw what was painted on the front.

Get In, Loser

"I know you don't have your place yet," she whispered, "but I know it's important for you to have your own home, and I wanted you to have something that could be just yours from the moment you walked in."

I pressed a kiss to that sexy mouth. "It's perfect and snarky and will remind me of you."

Color painted itself in streaks across her cheeks. "I wanted that, too." A beat. "Well, not to remind you of me by having you walk all over me, but because I—"

"I know, Rocky. Believe me, the last thing I want is to walk all over you." The vulnerability in her eyes made my heart clench again.

"I'm scared I'll start letting it happen," she whispered. "Like how it used to be with my family."

"Trust takes time to build," I said.

Her expression cleared. "Yeah, it does."

I bent a little so I could meet her eyes. "But we're building it."

Teeth pressing into her bottom lip, uncertainty creeping in, but then I watched her chin come up, her shoulders straighten. "Yes, we are."

I tucked her hair behind her ear. "Glad you see things the right way."

"The *right* way?" An arch look.

"The right way being *my* way."

She snorted. "Stop trying to make me mad enough so that I jump your bones again and open your other present."

"Oh, there will be jumping," I said.

"Out the window?" she asked sweetly.

I bopped her on the nose. "So long as it's a first-story one." I began unpeeling the tissue paper from the two cylindrical items in the box, grinned when I saw they were a pair of whiskey glasses.

"Happy housewarming," she murmured.

I carefully set the items on the coffee table, turned back and tugged her close, beyond touched that she'd gotten me a present at all, let alone several thoughtful items for my house. "Thank you, Rocky."

She shrugged. "It's nothing."

"Not to me," I said firmly.

Hope in her eyes. "I really like you, Hayden," she whispered.

My pulse picked up, so much affection for this woman in my bloodstream that I almost couldn't bear it. "Well, I *love* you, Anabelle."

Her breath caught. "Hay—"

Shit. I hadn't meant to say that. Not yet, anyway. Fingers to her lips. "Don't think about it."

"Don't"—she yanked her head back—"think about it? What's wrong with you? How could I not—"

I kissed her.

She bit my bottom lip.

"Ow!"

Solemn brown eyes on mine. "Do you mean it?"

I nodded. "Yeah, Rocky. I've been gone for you for a while."

"A while meaning the bare two weeks we've known each other?"

A shrug. "It's a McAlister thing."

"Insanity?"

"No." I slipped my arms around her, tugged her close. "Knowing a wonderful thing when we lay eyes on it, falling hard and fast and forever."

She released a shuddering breath. "I-I don't know if I'm there yet."

"That's okay," I said. "So long as you don't run just because I am. You're fucking incredible, Anabelle. That's just fact. You're funny and strong and smart and everything I could want. But . . . trust takes time. Relationships take time." I chucked her under the chin. "I promise my next gift won't be an engagement ring. Deal?"

Although, now I wasn't sure the other gift I had planned for her would go over all that well.

Kind of too late for that thought though.

"Deal." She swallowed hard then bit her lip again. "I do really like you," she murmured. "You know that, right?"

"Yeah, babe. I do." I freed that lip with a light brush of my thumb. "And it's enough, Rocky. I don't need anything more than time to keep building that trust. Hence the whole *don't think about it thing.*"

Another deep breath trailed by a small smile. "Okay." A beat paired with another slow inhale and exhale. Then, "Do you really like the presents?"

"I love them."

A bigger smile, shoulders relaxing. "Good."

"Why do you look like the cat ate the canary?"

She shrugged, nibbled at her bottom lip. "No reason."

I tickled her ribs. "Do I need to resort to this again?"

"No." She glared. "Plus, you'd better be careful, or I'll use my claws to get you." And with that, she tilted her head as though the hermit crab earrings were going to pinch me.

Laughing, I tucked her close, stealing a kiss, knowing I should get out of there and let her rest, that I'd thrown her a giant curveball and for all my talk of making her come and finding her bedroom, she needed more time. But . . . I just wanted a few more minutes with her.

"Hayden?"

"Hmm," I said, running my fingers through her hair. "I know you need to sleep."

"No." I glanced down.

"I was wondering why you weren't picking me up and carrying me down the hall."

A smirk curved my mouth. "Yeah?"

"Yeah." A shrug. "You're too big for me to carry."

I chuckled. "You calling me fat?"

"Yup."

Laughing, I scooped her up and started walking. There weren't *that* many doors at the end of the hall. I could figure it out. "So long as it's the P-H-A-T kind."

"Oh boy." She snorted. "I knew you wouldn't disappoint."

"With the bad jokes or because I've used my superb directional skills to deduce your bedroom is this way." I nodded down the hall.

"Neither." A careless shrug. "Both." Fingers crawling down my chest, slipping over my abs, stopping an inch above the button of my cargos. "Guess again," she purred, lips pressing to my throat, tongue darting out, a hot brand against my skin.

"My inability to guess what kind of movies you like?" I pushed open a door, saw it was the bathroom.

"Nope." Another giggle that made me feel about ten feet tall. "Also, I don't like movies."

I froze, glanced down at her. "Like at all?"

She bit her lip, shy creeping into her eyes. "I never had anyone who I wanted to go with."

"Well, that's going to change," I told her. "'Cause I just earned a permanent seat next to you."

She lifted a brow. "Permanent?"

"Yup." I shoved open another door, saw it was the bedroom, and thanked all the various gods in the universe.

"When you can't even guess my favorite cocktail?"

I dumped her onto the bed. "I know it," I admitted, having finally put the pieces together. No frou-frou stuff. Just— "Whiskey, on the rocks."

She blinked then smiled. "Damn, I knew the glasses would give it away."

"Gotta have good glasses to drink good whiskey."

"True."

I followed her down onto the mattress. "So," I said, nudging her legs apart, positioning myself in between.

Laughter slid from her eyes, heat taking its place. "So," she repeated, hands coming up to rest on my shoulders.

Bending, I ran my lips along her throat, pressed a kiss to her jaw.

"So . . . what's your favorite color?"

Still as a statue,

Then she began giggling.

And I knew this was going to be the best night—er, morning —of my life.

SEVENTEEN

Anabelle

I BARELY STOPPED GIGGLING before his mouth was pressed to mine, his tongue delving deep.

Desire replaced amusement in an instant, and I wrapped my legs around him, fingers clenching on his shoulders to pull him down. I wanted to feel the weight of his body against mine, revel in all the hard parts of him pressing to my soft. I wanted—

"Skin," I gasped when he kissed his way to my earlobe, tugged lightly with his teeth.

This was nice.

But I needed skin.

I slipped my fingers under the hem of his shirt, began tugging up, beyond thankful when Hayden reared back and wrenched it over his head. A second later, he was doing the same to my sweater, to the T-shirt I wore underneath.

But I was concentrating less on my body and much more on his.

Fuck, he was gorgeous. Strong, lean muscles lining his arms, his chest, faint squares on his abdomen, a light dusting of hair over his pecs.

My fingers itched to touch. Moisture pooled between my thighs.

A teasing caress over the tops of my breasts, tracing down and in between, dipping under the cotton of my bra.

Maybe once I would have felt self-conscious to just be me in the face of so much beauty, but that discomfort was negligible in this moment. All I had to do was look at Hayden, and I could see the desire on his face. Then there was the way he touched me, almost reverently, as though I were the most important thing in this moment.

And . . . I supposed I was.

Because, in this moment, he was equally important to me.

I ran my hands over his chest, palming the muscles, loving the slight prickle of the hair there against my skin, loving even more that as I touched him, he touched me. Fingers down my back, palm cupping my ass, sliding up and in so he could flick open the button on my jeans.

I covered his hand with mine.

"No?" he asked.

"Only if you take off yours first."

A grin, desire in those blue eyes, before he hopped off the bed and shucked his shoes, socks, and cargo pants.

I lifted my palm, face out when he moved to get back on the bed. "Wait."

"Rocky?"

"Just wait."

His expression gentled. "We don't have to do this—"

"Shh."

He stood there in all his sexy glory and I had to fight the urge to launch myself at him as I looked my fill.

A sigh.

My gaze drifted up his chest, met his. "You know, I don't make *everything* a fight," I murmured.

He took a step closer, and I could see the ridge of his erection cupped by the black cotton of his boxer briefs. "The current situation would state otherwise," he said dryly.

"I have an ulterior motive," I told him and made a circling motion with my finger. "Now spin."

A snort, but he spun around in a circle.

"Good God, that ass," I muttered. "The fates are just too cruel to give a man an ass like—*ack!*" I fought the urge to shut my eyes, instead drinking up every last inch of exposed skin when he dropped his boxer briefs to the carpet. "What are you doing?" I asked, eyes glued to his naked, gorgeous body.

"You're waxing poetic about my ass," he said, turning back around and putting one knee up on the bed. I figured I might as well give you the full view."

And what a fucking view it was.

"Smart-ass," I muttered.

He reached up and unzipped my pants, tugging them down my legs. Then he crawled up my body, pressed all that naked skin to mine. "*Nice* ass." Except, his hand was cupping my butt, massaging the curves. Then in a moment almost too fast for my brain to process, he flipped me, so I was face down on the mattress.

"Really fucking nice ass," he murmured, a palm on each cheek, kneading lightly through the simple cotton of my underwear. But even without fancy lingerie—side note: I needed to buy some—the sensation was incredible. Warm, rough hands on mine, massaging slow and deep, sending tendrils of pleasure weaving through me. And his words upped the ante. "You don't know how many dreams I've had about this thing. Watching it bounce as you walked away from me, seeing it sway as you stretched up high for a bottle of booze."

My breathing wasn't steady in the least, but I managed to say, "You haven't had time to have lots of dreams."

"Oh, Rocky," he whispered, and I felt his hot breath just above my ass, the words glazing my skin like frosting. "You underestimate my imagination."

A kiss above the hook of my bra, making my breath hitch.

"It's not imagination," I pushed out.

A chuckle, the clasp popping open. "Okay, dreaming ability then."

"Is that—" I broke off for a moment when those calloused hands slipped under the band, pushing the straps off my shoulders. "Another of your super, secret agent skills?"

"Hmm?" he asked, hands brushing up and down my back.

Goose bumps prickled on my skin, my nerve endings on fire. When this man touched me, every cell seemed to come alive. And when he followed the trail of his fingers with his mouth, pressing gentle teasing kisses to my nape, all down my spine, desire pooled between my thighs, the ache to have him inside growing more intense with every second.

Still, I liked bantering with him, even in this setting, and so I managed to prompt, "Your dreaming ability?"

A rough chuckle. "I have no idea what you're talking about," he said against my skin.

"I—"

He kissed me, just shifted my head slightly so he could take my lips in a searing kiss that knocked all thoughts of banter out of my brain.

"What did you mean, Rocky?" he asked when he pulled back.

My chest was heaving, my skin seeming tight and too small for my body.

And I couldn't remember what I'd meant. Something about

skills and dreams, but mostly all I could think was how good it felt when Hayden had his hands on me.

"I don't care anymore."

Another chuckle, and I swear this one arrowed right toward my pussy, it was so full of rough, male heat. Then he slid his palms beneath me to cup my breasts.

We both groaned, and when his thumb brushed my nipple, I bucked. "Hayden!"

A smile against my skin, a nip to my shoulder, and in one of those rapid movements, he flipped me again. I bounced once before he was on me again, this time tugging my bra off and tossing it to the side, his head dipping to take my nipple into his mouth.

Oh, fuck, that was good.

Pleasure tore through me, tightened every muscle, and I found my hands in his hair, holding him to me.

A palm sliding down, nudging my panties off my hips, down my thighs, fingers slipping between. He groaned against my breasts the moment he encountered the wet folds of my pussy.

"Fuck, baby," he whispered. "You're so wet."

"More," I demanded, tugging on his hair, wanting his mouth on my nipples, even as he stroked his finger around the entrance to my body.

He bent and sucked my other nipple deep, thumb shifting so it brushed my clit, alternating between circling it and pressing firmly, finding the rhythm I liked best and then exploiting it with those secret skills until I felt every cell in my body come to life. Pleasure built, need coiling in my abdomen, spreading outward, as I wound tighter and tighter and tighter until—

"Hayden!" I gasped as I exploded.

Lips on my nipple, suckling, wringing every last bit of desire out of my body until I collapsed limply back to the mattress.

Only then did he release my breast, slip his fingers free.

He shifted to the side, one warm hand resting on my stomach, tracing light patterns on my skin.

"I hope you're not planning on stopping," I said, my tone missing my usual sharp, mostly because he'd just pleasured it out of me.

"Oh, no," he murmured, mouth brushing mine. "I'm not that good."

"You better not be," I whispered and wrapped my arms around his shoulders, kissing him with every bit of like—and maybe more—that I possessed. "Give me everything, Hayden. I want to see every part of you." I reached down, wrapped my fingers around his hard cock. "To *feel* every part."

And it was like a leash had snapped.

He rolled to his back, taking me with him so I was on top, his hands touching every inch of me he could reach, his mouth demanding as his tongue rubbed against mine in a tempo that had me blowing past the limpness that had settled into my limbs after my orgasm. Need rocketed through me, making my pussy ache, my nipples bead into hard little points.

But even with all of that, I needed so much more.

I needed everything.

Pumping my hand up and down the hard length of him, I started to shift down to take him inside.

He groaned when the head of his cock brushed my pussy, hips jerking.

"Wait, baby," he whispered. "Condom."

Fuck. Condom. Of course, we needed a condom. Except . . . I didn't have any. It wasn't like my sex life was rocking, and I'd been quite clear on my only-buying-things-that-I-needed hang-up.

First thing tomorrow I was going to do was buy some.

"I'm clean," he said. "I was tested before I got out."

"I'm on the shot," I told him. "But I haven't been tested in a while. We should—"

A nod, another quick movement, and he was out from beneath me, reaching for his pants and extracting his wallet. He had a condom in his hand, rolled it down the length of his cock, and was prowling back toward me in just a few seconds.

I lay back, spread my legs, not missing the heavy weight of his gaze nor the way it made me feel as it traced every inch of me.

"You don't want to assume the previous position?" he asked, crawling up the length of my body, stopping only to press a kiss to my ankle, my calf, the inside of my thigh.

"No," I breathed, the exhale shuddering out when he paused between my legs and traced his tongue up through the damp heat. A flick against my clit that had me seeing stars, my fingers threading into his hair. I tugged upward, but he didn't move; Instead . . .

He gave me the best kiss of my life.

Tongue tracing and flicking, delving inside, his thumb coming to my clit. Then switching hand and mouth, one finger pressing into me while he nipped and kissed and used the flat of his tongue against the sensitive bundle of nerves.

Stars at the edges of my vision, tension coiling in my limbs, heat licking at my nerve endings, and then—

He pulled away.

"Hayden!"

A grin, cocky and sexy as hell, but before I could snap at him for it, he was moving up my body, pushing inside.

"Fuck," he groaned. "That's good."

I agreed, but couldn't form words, not with need filling me, not with my eyes rolling into the back of my head, not with my fingers clenching on the hard planes of his chest, his back, his stomach, my hips thrusting against him as he slid out and then back in.

Not when pleasure was already spreading through me.

Not when—

He began moving.

In and out. Pressing deep, sliding back *oh so slowly*. I couldn't do anything except feel.

"More," I gasped when he started stroking faster, hitting just the right spot, the right rhythm. It wasn't a struggle, and there wasn't any hesitation. It was just Hayden and me and the easy drumbeat of us together.

As though we'd been meant for each other from the moment we'd been created.

As though we'd just needed our voices to mix on that porch, our bodies to connect at the bar, our hearts to become laced together on the beach and everything would be right in the world.

He cupped my breast, slanted his mouth over mine, shifted his hips so he pressed against my clit on every thrust . . . and that was it.

I exploded, my orgasm bursting through me in a cloud sparkling pleasure, making my lips tingle, my fingertips prickle, my skin tighten further as wave after wave of bliss coursed through my body.

Distantly, I felt Hayden stroke into me once, twice more, before he groaned and collapsed, his lips against my throat, his limp body heavy on mine.

The soft words he whispered in my ear weren't distant, however. I heard them with crystal clarity, held them close to my heart, in a safe place I knew would never be breached.

"I love you, Rocky."

And I almost said it back.

The feeling was there. In my heart, my gut, my brain.

But . . . I was too scared. So instead, I held him close, arms and legs wrapped tightly around him, as both of our breathing slowed, as our pulses steadied, as sleep crept up and over me.

THE RINGING WASN'T WELCOME.

Really. Not. Fucking. Welcome.

I rolled to the side, grabbed my phone and saw it was my brother calling.

A thread of worry had me swiping my finger across the screen, had me bringing it up to my ear, and saying, "Hello?" softly as I tried to extract myself from Hayden's hold.

He'd rolled with me toward the phone, but now he was playing octopus, a heavy arm around my waist, his legs pinning mine to the bed.

"Anabelle," my brother clipped out. "We need to talk."

I stiffened, alarm coursing through me. "Is Dad okay?"

"He's fine," Tom said. "For now. But you need to consider that what you're doing with your life isn't good for him."

"For him?" I asked. "Or for you?"

No hesitation before his response. "For him. You already killed one of our parents—"

"No." I sat up, knew that in the short length of time since the conversation began, Hayden had fully woken because he didn't fight the motion, just sat up next to me and pressed his shoulder to mine.

"No, what?" Tom snapped.

I sucked in a breath, released it slowly. "No, you don't get to use that anymore. I hate that she's gone. I miss her more than you would believe." Another breath. "But I'm done with taking on whatever guilt it is that you're displacing onto me. I don't know if I'm an easy target, or if you're shouldering your own guilt and so it's easier for you to blame me, but I'm done being your punching bag."

Not even a beat between me finishing that speech and his response. "It's your fau—"

"No," I repeated. "It's not."

A pause this time, probably expecting me to cave or apologize or make nice. I might have done it before, just to get the conversation over with, to avoid having to dig any additional heavy emotions up.

Except . . . they were already up.

They were already pressing on both of us. "We used to be close once," I said. "I miss those times. I want us to find our way back to that."

Only cold in reply. "You're the one who left."

"You're right. I did. But I'm not in the habit of running from my life anymore," I said, then added quickly, just to make my intentions clear, "That doesn't mean I'm switching coasts like you guys did. I like it here in California. I have a life, a job. But I'll talk to Dad, let him know I'll visit more regularly. That I won't disappear."

"Your job—"

"Is not up for discussion," I said. "I don't know that I'll do it long term or go back to school or become a fucking receptionist at a nudist colony. What I *do* know? Is that if you give one damn about me as your sister—and I think you do, based on the fact that for all the crap you've piled on me over the years you've never cut me out of your life—then you need to stop treating me like shit."

Silence.

"Because that's why I never severed ties, Tom. That's why I visit." I sighed. "I love you guys. That won't change. *Ever*. I just . . . need to find my own path. One that's mine alone."

Quiet. So much quiet that I thought for a second he'd actually hung up, but then I glanced down at my cell and saw the call was still going.

I put it back up to my ear just in time to hear him sigh.

"A nudist colony?" he asked. "Really?"

Amusement made my lips curve. "If I want."

I could almost hear him shaking his head, but then he sighed, and his voice went warmer than I'd heard in years, almost reminiscent of my big brother growing up. "I need to think on what you said." A beat, then, "I never considered—" He broke off.

"Tom."

He kept going. "If I'm doing what you said, if it's something I'm holding on to, that I'm blaming you for and have no right to, then . . . I'm sorry," he said. "But you know I'm not great with emotions, at looking deeply at them when they don't involve work—"

"Your work involves emotions?" I teased.

"Occasionally." Another sigh. "I don't deviate off courses well, but you brought up a valid argument. I'll look into it. I promise you."

Not soft, fluffy words. Not statements of affection.

But an apology and a promise to look into himself.

So, in the end, it was much more than I expected.

"Think you can convince Kelly to stop trying to intervene in my life as well?"

Tom snorted. "No," he said. "Did you know the other day, she came over while Betty"—his wife—"and I were at work and changed out all the sheets in the house?"

"Considering the same brand of sheets are on my bed because she made me FaceTime her while I changed them or else she'd fly out and put them on herself? Yes." I laughed, hope and joy bubbling in my heart when he laughed alongside me. "Thankfully, they are nice sheets."

"Yes," he said. "There is that."

"And you still think I should come home and subject myself to the power of Kelly?"

Silence. "We all miss you."

A hard thump in my chest, one that gave me the hope that things might get better. Not go back to the way they were, but that we might find a new way forward. "I promise I'll visit soon."

A chuckle. "Drawing the line in the sand already?"

"Yup."

"Good," he said, surprising me. "Anabelle—"

Hayden's phone beeped and he murmured a quiet, "Sorry," before slipping from the bed and going over to answer it.

"Was that a man?" Tom demanded, voice hardening. "Do you have a man in your house? It's early. Does that mean you had a man spend the night?"

"Newsflash, I'm not a virgin, bro," I said, glancing over at Hayden, seeing his lips twitch upward as he slipped into the hall to finish his call.

"I—"

"Gotta go," I said and hung up before he could say anything further. Before either of us got mad enough to ruin the progress we'd just made.

My phone buzzed before it reached my lap.

I'm sorry. I promise I'll do some thinking and figure it out.

Lungs easing, I shook my head, started typing out a response, but before I could, my cell vibrated again.

And he'd better treat you right, or he'll have to answer to me.

Another text came through almost immediately.

I know what right is.

Because I also know I've been doing it wrong for all these years.

I was blinking back an annoying itch in my eyes—definitely not tears, no ma'am—when Hayden walked back into the room.

"You okay?" he asked, immediately coming to my side.

I nodded.

"You were fucking fabulous," he said, cupping my cheeks in his palms. "I am so, *so* proud of you for saying that. For being strong and articulate and"—he waggled his brows—"for wanting to work at a nudist colony. I'm in. Sign me up."

Snorting, I dropped my forehead to his shoulder, so many feelings for this man welling up inside me, coalescing into a bigger, deeper emotion.

Into love.

So much love that I wanted to shout it from the rooftops, to kiss Hayden senseless and tell him I must have a little McAlister in me because I'd fallen for him, too.

But before I could, he scooped me into his arms and carried me into the bathroom.

The shower was already running, steam filling the space.

"Wash up," he murmured, "and I promise, I'll cook you breakfast."

"You saying I smell?" He put his nose to my armpit and inhaled as I shrieked and tried to block him. "Hayden!"

"You smell like the most fucking delicious treat on the planet, but I have a job interview this morning and I want to feed you first." Hay brushed his thumb over my bottom lip. "Let me?"

"A job interview?"

He nodded. "KTS set it up. A security company that works with them remotely."

"That sounds—"

He kissed me. "Perfect," he whispered, "because you thought of it. Thank you." Another press of his mouth to mine.

"Congratulations," I said when he pulled away.

"I haven't gotten the job yet." His thumb brushed my bottom lip, sent heat arrowing between my thighs.

But he had a chance, so I stepped back when I wanted to move forward, to request a repeat of the last hours. "You will."

Gentle eyes, amazing words. "I love you."

My lips parted, but before I could say anything, he nudged me toward the shower and slipped out the door. "I hope you like pancakes," he called, voice fading as he moved away.

"Only if they're chocolate chip!" I called back.

"Are there any other kind?" he hollered.

I laughed, filled with so much happiness that it expanded within me, threatening to burst and consume me.

But that was okay.

Because I found that being happy with Hayden in my life wasn't half bad.

Hell, who was I kidding?

It was incredible, and I wasn't letting him go.

EIGHTEEN

Hayden

I STROLLED up to Anabelle's door the next day, a sheaf of papers in my hand, and rang the doorbell.

Footsteps echoed through the wooden panel and then the door was pulled open. She leaned against the frame, crossed her arms, and lifted one brow. "No doorbell ditch this time?"

"Nope." I bent and kissed her. "Not when we have good cooking just minutes away."

Anabelle grinned. "Fair point." She inclined her head. "Come in, I just need to get my jacket."

My phone rang just as I stepped into the hall, and I set the papers down in order to pull my cell from my pocket. "Hello?" I said, after swiping my finger across its screen and putting it up to my ear.

"Hello, Hayden," the woman who interviewed me the previous day said.

"Dominique," I said. "Hi, how are you?"

"Great," she replied, not bothering to ask how I was doing in turn. Even if it was mostly an American thing to ask that question, Dominique was very much no-nonsense, to say the least. "A job offer is hitting your inbox shortly. If you accept, you start Monday."

"I might need a little more time to get my utilities and computer set up."

"Your house closed today, I'll send a team over the weekend with the proper equipment and to take care of the utilities."

Efficient, but I guessed I shouldn't have expected anything less. "Okay," I said. "I guess I'll review the offer and be ready to start Monday."

"Okay."

"Great, thanks, Dominique," I said, "Good—"

She hung up before I could finish the reply, but that was okay because I had a job. One that would keep me here with my sister, my friends, my Rocky, but one that allowed me to still help people.

And speaking of my Rocky, she was leaning against the wall that led into the kitchen, her arms crossed, a smile on her face.

I pocketed my cell, closed the distance between us.

"Is Dominique an ex-girlfriend?" she teased.

"No," I said with a shudder. "I like my women strong, but I prefer that they have a *little* give."

"What does that mean?"

"Only that I'm not sure that Dominique is anything but ice."

Anabelle smiled and tsked. "Oh, you poor man. Have you learned nothing?" she asked. When I frowned, she added, "The ice is just there to hide all of the pain and insecurity."

I froze. "Damn, you're smart, Rocky."

"Yup." She let her body rest against mine. "So, you got the job?"

"Yeah."

Her smile took my breath away. "That's so awesome, Hay. I'm proud of you."

"Your doing," I said. "I wouldn't have thought of it if you hadn't suggested doing something remote."

"Remember the whole *smart* thing?" she teased, rubbing her nose against mine. "Now, come on," she said, tugging me toward the door. "Let's go get fat at Iris's house. I want to eat all the things."

"There's that smart again," I joked, following her.

She snorted.

"Oh, hold on," I said. "I just need to get my papers."

She was closer to the table and turned to snag the folder, but I'd turned, too, and we ended up bumping into each other, the papers flying to the floor.

"Shoot." She dropped to her knees.

I did the same, not wanting her to see, not when I had a whole speech I'd intended to give her, along with these papers.

Except . . . she'd already grabbed one, and it was the one that happened to be the most important.

The first page of the paperwork I'd signed the previous day, a meeting I'd rushed to after the interview with Dominque, one that meant I'd closed on my house much sooner than I'd planned.

Which was actually the house in front of this little cottage.

The address that I could see her lips forming.

"Your house?" she whispered and cut her eyes to the open front door. "That house?"

"Baby," I began, "I was going to tell you. I wanted—"

She put her hand up, cutting me off, her chest rising and falling on a deep exhale as her eyes slid closed.

"Rocky."

The only response I received was a shake of her head.

And that was the moment I realized I'd made a major

miscalculation. I'd figured I'd tell her it was a way for us to get closer, but we could still have the space to take our time, that this way she wouldn't have to move from the place she loved, that if things worked out (not that I had any intention of them *not* working out) then we would have an easy way to take the next step.

But I didn't get a chance to say any of that.

Because she burst to her feet and darted out the front door.

The last thing I saw was the end of her long black ponytail flapping behind her as she sprinted away.

———

STUNNED, raw, kicking myself six ways to Sunday, I let Anabelle run for far too long—okay, it was maybe half a minute at the most before I got my shit together and I realized what in the fuck I was letting her do.

Leaving the papers, I stood and hustled out the front door.

I'd catch up to her. I'd explain. I'd make it all right.

Hell, I could keep living with Brooke and Kace until she was comfortable letting me move in and—

I turned the corner to the front of the house and felt my heart seize.

Because she was running back.

She stopped two inches in front of me, opened her mouth.

I beat her to it. "I'm sorry," I said. "I had a whole plan to explain it. This isn't me trying to trap you. I just know you loved the house and it was in my budget and close to you and Brooke and Brent. And I didn't want you to have to move and I wanted to surprise you and—"

She tossed her arms around my neck and kissed me.

"I know," she said when she broke away, her breaths coming in rapid gusts against my lips. "I can't deny that I freaked out.

But I got to my car and realized that aside from not having my keys"—a wry smile—"I also didn't have something else important."

"Your backpack?" I asked lightly, heart thumping, but hope a growing thread inside me. She'd come back. She'd kissed me. Those pretty brown eyes were free of panic now.

"That," she murmured. "And you." Her hands came up and cupped my cheeks. "You wonderful, thoughtful, sweet, *pushy* man."

"I didn't mean to push."

"You did," she said, still smiling. "But that's okay. Because we have something good and wonderful and incredible, and it needs to be pushed to grow. I want to find out what kind of happiness you and I can find together."

"You do?"

She nodded. "I do." A beat. "So, you'll live in the front and I'll stay at my place, and we'll have regular sleepovers until you can convince me that you need a roommate."

I chuckled. "I love you."

"I know." A grin. "Just like I know you'll probably push me into the house so that you can use my cottage as an office."

Now *that* was a thought.

She smacked me lightly on the chest. "Don't even think about it," she ordered, eyes narrowed. "I'll only accept *some* pushy, not all of it."

"You like my pushy."

"Lies." A sniff.

I didn't call her on her lie. I didn't tease her back.

Instead, I scooped her up in my arms, dropped my lips to hers, and kissed her with all the love and hope and need inside me.

The best part?

She kissed me back.

"I'm sorry," I said a few hours after I'd carried Anabelle inside and had shown her just how much it meant to me for her to kiss me back.

We'd gotten to Iris and Brent's late enough that they'd texted to say they were going to eat without us, and had, in fact, eaten without us. The only plus to Iris's dark look, to her super-mean-glarey-eyes as Anabelle had deemed them, was that Iris had saved us plates, had even kept them warm in the oven.

I'd take glaring upon arriving two hours late to dinner if it meant I could have a happy and pleasured Anabelle at my side, along with Iris's chicken pot pie in my stomach.

But a few moments ago, Iris had produced a pair of glasses very similar to the ones Anabelle had bought me then comman-deered the bottle of whiskey I'd brought, telling me the girls were going to drink to my new house—and then she and Anabelle had shooed the "boys" out onto the back deck.

It was too cold for a BBQ, but I appreciated the females' intervention. It was beyond time Brent and I officially hashed things out.

I needed to get through the grudge so we could move forward.

Hence the *I'm sorry*.

Brent shrugged. "We've always been square, dude."

I shifted in my seat. "Then why have you been giving me the silent treatment?"

A roll of his eyes as the back door slid open. "Man, when have I ever given *anyone* the silent treatment?"

Iris emerged, carrying two beers and coughed at his words. To Brent's credit, he didn't even glance at his woman, just pointed a finger and shushed her.

She smacked a kiss to his cheek. "Nice try," she murmured.

"But that doesn't work on me." Her gaze flicked to mine. "He was upset. He got over it. He's ready to move on."

Brent sighed.

"Am I wrong?" she pressed.

He made a face. "No."

"Exactly."

She passed over the two beers. "Enjoy these then come into the kitchen in fifteen."

"Sure that timer is set, darlin'?"

Horror in her blue-green eyes. "You didn't."

Brent just smiled evilly.

"So much trouble," Iris said on a huff, hurrying inside.

"Did you mess with the timer?" I asked when the door had closed behind her.

"Fuck, no," Brent said, opening a beer and handing it to me. "I learned my lesson the hard way."

"What was the hard way?" I asked, genuinely curious.

A sigh as the other beer cracked open. "You really want to know?"

"I wouldn't have asked if I didn't."

Another sigh. "You laugh, and I'll punch you in the junk."

"I'll laugh if I want and block you if you try."

Brent grinned, took a swig of his beer. "Bastard."

"Takes one to know one."

"Glad you're back."

My lungs froze for a heartbeat, but then I forced myself to nod as though I hadn't been hoping to hear something like that from him for weeks. I hadn't expected it, had still thought it would take a lot more time. But, fuck he was a good friend. "Me, too," I said. "I missed you and your dumb ass."

"At least my ass is nice and squeezable."

"I resent that comment. Anabelle thinks *my* ass is perfect."

"Can't account for taste."

I punched him in the shoulder. He punched me back.

Then Brent told me the story of Iris's timers and her cherry pie.

I laughed my ass off . . . and successfully blocked Brent from punching me in the junk. But it felt good to be sitting with my friend, laughing about good memories, giving each other shit. It made the last ten years seem worth it, made me appreciate him and our relationship so much more than I'd ever thought possible.

And when he gave me shit about not knowing Anabelle's favorite color, I just laughed and dished it back.

For the first time in my adult life, I had time to figure my life out. I had a future and plans and exciting things to learn and tackle. I was . . . just so damned glad I was back where I belonged.

Plus, when the timer went off fifteen minutes later and we all sat down to pie, I learned that Iris was right. Her cherry pie was the absolute shit.

Still couldn't understand why Brent would want to burn it though.

EPILOGUE

PART ONE

Anabelle, Three Months Later

I STILL HADN'T SAID it.

Hadn't said those terrifying three little words. *I. Love. You.*

Why? Stupidity.

At first, I'd been too scared. Then I'd wanted it to be special, to not just blurt it out, but to have it mean something and be poignant and romantic and—

Now, it was a huge elephant in the room.

I'd given up on romantic, on poignant, and so every day I was fighting the urge to just blurt it out and get it over with. But every time I tried, I got all tongue-twisted and nervous and instead said something else from nice to teasing to snarky to downright weird.

Hell, last night I'd actually all but shouted, "I love you . . . r banana!"

What the actual fuck, am I right?

I mean, I liked his banana, loved it actually, almost as much as I loved him.

Problem was, I was beginning to think that I would never be able to say it.

I'd just be yelling random things like "I love you . . . r shoelaces!" or "I love you . . . r wine bottle opener thingy!" for eternity.

Well, no. I wasn't going to let that happen.

No ma'am. No way. No how.

I had a plan. I was going to say, "I love you" and he was going to . . . well, *love* it.

Just that easy.

With a determined lift to my chin, I strode through our backyard and onto the back deck. I hadn't moved in with him yet, his office was still inside. Well, he *thought* it was still inside.

But that was part of the plan.

I'd packed my stuff. I'd finagled a phone call with the elusive Dominique. Brooke and Kace had distracted Hayden for the day.

And now, he had a state-of-the-art office in *our* backyard studio.

I juggled the box in my hands, carefully left it on the top step of the wrap-around porch he'd added onto the house.

Then I ran and hid.

He'd texted, saying he was only five minutes out, and I'd gotten my ass in gear.

Even now, I heard his car pull up in front of the house, the driver's door slam shut, footsteps approaching the side gate. I'd been paying attention to everything about this man, knew his routine.

When he came home, he entered through the side gate, dropped his things on the porch and then always came to my studio to greet me properly.

Didn't matter if he'd been gone for fifteen minutes or all day, if I was in the studio, he came to see me first. And I'd made sure to let him know I was in the studio . . . even though I'd run and hidden in the shadows of his favorite spying tree the moment after I'd dropped the box on his porch.

It really did give a nice view of our doors.

Rocks crunched, and Hayden appeared around the corner of the house. His eyes immediately went to the box, his stride faltering for a beat before smoothing out as he continued over to it. God, he was gorgeous, and even more so when I watched him smile and shake his head, heard him mutter something about a "troublesome, wonderful woman"—no clue who that could be, *grin*—and then I held my breath as he opened the box.

It was another doormat.

Only this one read,

The McAlisters

His eyes darted up, seeming to see me in my hiding place behind the tree, but I was already slipping out, already moving toward him.

Three steps away, and I could see the emotion blazing in the deep blue depths of his eyes.

Two steps. My throat tightened.

One step. My mouth opened, and I yelled, "I love you!"

Yup. Yelled.

Shouted it right in his face. No warning. Just silent to screaming.

Hayden set the box down, took me in his arms. "I know, Rocky," he murmured, holding me tight. "I know. It's okay."

I sniffed, nodded, relief loosening my throat. "I love you," I repeated, much more sedately.

"I love you, too, baby." He leaned back, lightly brushed his lips over mine. "I have from the moment I laid eyes on you, and I won't stop until my heart is no longer beating."

"Fuck, you're good," I whispered.

He laughed. I laughed, and then I kissed him, held him

tight, tucked those words down and gave him the same words back over and over again, until we were both out of breath, until my mouth felt swollen, until need was coiled heavy and tight in my abdomen.

And just because I finally could, I said it one more time.

"I love you."

His eyes were soft and warm, his expression adoring, and I felt so damned lucky to have him in my life.

Although, not so lucky as to not risk teasing him.

Because that was a different kind of luck, wasn't it? Having a person you could be heavy with one moment, could joke with the next.

"You ready for a roommate?" I asked lightly.

He grinned, brushed his lips against mine. "I thought you'd never ask. When am I moving in?"

I snorted, smacked him lightly. "Come on," I ordered. "I have some boxes for you to move."

He chuckled and pinched my butt even as he followed me to the cottage.

And then I got to surprise him for the second time.

I opened the door and showed him his new office.

"Fuck, I love you," he said a minute later, after he managed to find his voice. He turned, sweeping me up, holding me close, and carrying me to the only piece of horizontal furniture in the space.

The couch.

It was second-hand. It was a little hard and had the occasional sharp edge that would stab anyone who sat on it. But it was loved, and soft spots could be found. It might be a little damaged and a whole lot worn down, but it could be given a new life.

I wasn't much for analogies, but damn if that wasn't the perfect one.

EPILOGUE
PART TWO

Dominique

I DIDN'T KNOW what in the fuck I was doing in a bar at midnight on a weeknight.

Not sleeping.

Not getting drunk.

Not working.

Not doing anything aside from nursing the single beer that Hayden's girlfriend had pulled for me several hours ago.

And staring at myself in the mirror behind the bar, wondering how in the world I'd gotten to this place.

Less in an at-the-actual-bar question and more of a what-the-fuck-was-I-doing-with-my-life sort of way. I'd built connections in the world of private military operations. I took down bad guys on the regular with hardly more than my computer and my wits.

But . . . I didn't have that.

That being what the rest of this fucking bar composed almost entirely of lovebirds had.

Love.

Multiple different groups of couples in the booths in the back, all lovey-dovey and cuddling nonstop—something I'd witnessed many times over in the last hours since Hayden had dragged me here after one of our few in-person meetings.

We'd needed to devise a strategy to take down a ring of hackers trying to sell people's personal information, a really fucking sneaky ring, and sometimes that meant having to look outside the box . . . or the secure chat window that was my preferred mode of contact.

Look, I *could* schmooze and be charming and woo new clients, just as easily as I could hack through someone's firewall.

But two guesses as to which I preferred.

And it really better only take one.

Anyway, I knew I should have left hours before, but something had made me stay. Maybe the handsome black bartender who'd swept his beautiful blond girlfriend up into a kiss when she'd brought him a plate of cookies—and yes, I was good enough at my job to know that the bartender was Brent and his fiancé was Iris. I'd done a full background on Hayden before I hired him, including his sister and her boyfriend, Kace, who owned the bar. All of whom were spending the majority of their time mooning over their significant others. Hayden to the pretty and spunky Anabelle, who I quite liked and seemed to alternate between faux annoyance with Hayden and love shining in those deep brown eyes. Since annoyance was an emotion I readily identified with, I could at least support *that* type of mooning. On the other hand, Kace and Brooke were sickening.

Brooke was too damned cute with her pencil behind one ear, her eyes focused on her laptop, her red hair askew, but she and Kace seemed to orbit one another.

She shifted unconsciously in her seat when he was near, even though her fingers didn't stop. He didn't interrupt, just pressed a kiss over the top of her head, brushing his knuckles over her cheek, her nape, her arm, filling the glass in front of her with soda at regular intervals.

Love. Caring for one another. Instinctive.

Fucking fairytales under neon bar signs.

"Here," a silken male voice said.

Ignoring the way that voice slid over my skin, as though he were running a piece of delicate silk over my naked body, I glanced up into a pair of stunning hazel eyes. The different shades of green and gold and brown mixed together in a way that was both beautiful and completely unique.

But I didn't react on the outside.

First, I'd seen plenty of beautiful men in my life. Second, I'd felt him approach, but since he'd spent the vast majority of the night well away from me, I hadn't bothered to look too closely.

Not a threat. Moving on.

Now, I glanced down to see the drink in front of me. An orange and red concoction with a cherry floating on top of some ice cubes. A cheery red straw was perched on the side.

"What's this?" I asked.

He rolled those gorgeous, unique eyes, and I actually felt my skin prickle in awareness. "Sex on the Beach."

"Excuse me?" It was an arched question that sent amusement tap-dancing through his expression.

"Their"—he nodded at a group of couples hovering near his end of the bar—"ladies' night was apparently crashed by their husbands. Now they're enjoying ordering the dirtiest cocktails they can think of and having the men pay the tab. I mixed one too many and figured you could use something that wasn't warm beer."

I ran my finger through the condensation on the outside of the glass. "And Sex on the Beach was the dirtiest they could think of?"

"Apparently." He nudged it closer. "Have a sip. Despite the

cheesy name, it's actually pretty good." He nodded at my beer. "And since you don't seem to be enjoying your beer . . ."

"I'm not much of a beer girl."

"What kind of girl are you?"

Uh-oh.

The way he said that, with the quiet note of heat hidden beneath silk, was troublesome. Even more troublesome was my body's reaction.

Moisture pooled between my thighs. My nipples went tingly.

Nope. Not gonna do it.

I lifted my chin. "First of all, I'm a woman, not a girl."

Hazel eyes dipped down before returning to mine, a slow smile curving his mouth. That smile was . . .

Fucking hell.

I shifted on my barstool, thighs clenching together because . . . that smile was pure, unadulterated sex.

On the seats.

An image of him spreading my legs, of those broad shoulders pushing my thighs wide as he pressed those lush lips to my pussy made the alarm bells transform into hurricane sirens.

Because I was imagining having sex on the seats.

With a stranger.

With a stranger I wanted more than I wanted my careful distance.

Oh. *Shit.*

—Sex On The Seats coming 2021

SEX ON THE SHEETS

Preorder your copy at www.books2read.com/sexontheseats
Coming April 26th, 2021

LOVE AFTER MIDNIGHT

Rum And Notes

Virgin Daiquiri

On The Rocks

Sex On The Seats

LOVE AFTER MIDNIGHT

.

Did you miss any of the Love After Midnight Books? See below
for sneak peeks at the series and
check out www.elisefaber.com/loveaftermidnight for more
information!
And don't forget to signup for my newsletter for ALL the
release information http://eepurl.com/bdnmEj

Rum And Notes
Book 1
www.books2read.com/RumAndNotes

Brooke

"WANT A FRESH ONE?"

My eyes flew up from the glass to meet Kace's.

"Um," I murmured. "Sure. But can you add a little rum?"

A flash of white teeth. "All done, then?" He leaned toward me, resting his forearms on the bar, the long sleeves of his shirt riding up to reveal just the edge of a tattoo. I'd seen the whole tat before. On Day 36. He'd worn short sleeves for a change, a bone thrown to the unseasonably hot weather that day, and suddenly my hero had gotten tattoos, beautiful swirling lines crawling along his skin, sweeping around and up his forearms, twisting together and disappearing under the cotton of his short sleeves, tempting a woman to trace them with her tongue.

No.

My heroine's tongue.

Fantasy was fine, so long as I kept it between the pages.

I bit my bottom lip until the mental image faded, kept my tongue firmly in my mouth, and nodded at Kace.

He rapped his knuckles against the counter once, reciprocated my nod, then snagged my glass and turned away, dumping the contents, adding ice, rum, then soda before coming back over to me. He plunked the drink on the bar, but when I went to reach for it, he rested his hand on mine. "What are you working on so diligently?" he asked, and the contact, paired with his eyes locked on mine, stole my breath.

"Wh-what?"

His response was to release my hand, and while I was mourning the loss of his touch, he grabbed my computer, spun it to face him, and opened it.

"No—"

But it was too late.

It was open, the screen lighting up, illuminating his sharp but beautiful features, and he was reading.

Oh fuck, he was reading!

I made a mad grab for the laptop, but he swept it off the bar, lifting it in the air and continuing to read. My computer obscured most of his face, but not his eyebrows. Those brows kept rising until they were tight sideways C's on his forehead, well above the edge of my screen.

Then he lowered the laptop and stared at me.

"*This* is what you've been writing?"

In fairness, he'd caught me in the middle of a hot scene, made hotter because he'd been my inspiration for it.

A fact he seemed to understand when his eyes met mine. "Jace?"

I coughed. "It's a common name."

"Blue eyes?" He glanced back at the screen. "Tats? Brown hair?"

"Not an uncommon combination." I picked up my glass, drained it, eyes watering against the burn.

"A scar on the right side of his bottom lip?" he asked, putting my laptop down.

Okay, *now* was the time for running.

Something I normally abhorred, but in this case, it was critical. I snatched up my computer, reached into my wallet and pulled out some cash, and tossed it on the bar.

Then I jumped off the stool and ran.

—Rum And Notes (books2read.com/RumAndNotes)

Virgin Daiquiri
Book 2
www.books2read.com/VirginDaiquiri

Brent

Fuck. Someone needed to save this woman from herself.

That someone couldn't be me.

But that still didn't stop me from snagging her arm and rotating her to face me. "You live near the city now. You have to be smart." Her lips parted again, probably to tell me she *was* smart, but I kept talking. "*Street* smart. You can't tell strange men you live alone *or* invite them back to your place."

"Fine," she said.

"Fine," I agreed.

But I didn't let her go.

Her eyes flicked over my shoulder, to the ceiling, and my gaze followed hers, half-expecting to see a giant spider dangling there.

Instead, I saw mistletoe.

I glanced back down. She licked her lips.

And suddenly, I knew she was thinking the same thing as me. Warm bodies pressed together, lips only inches apart, heat filling the space, and a kiss-inducing plant overhead.

"Mistletoe," she whispered and licked her lips again.

Just one taste.

I could give myself that.

I bent my head and slanted my mouth across hers.

—Virgin Daiquiri (books2read.com/VirginDaiquiri)

ALSO BY ELISE FABER

On The Rocks (September 27th, 2020)

Sex On The Seats (April 2021)

Gold Hockey (all stand alone)

Blocked

Backhand

Boarding

Benched

Breakaway

Breakout

Checked

Coasting

Centered

Charging (December 28th, 2020)

Caged (March 2021)

Life Sucks Series (all stand alone)

Train Wreck

Hot Mess

Dumpster Fire (February 15th, 2021)

Roosevelt Ranch Series (all stand alone, series complete)

Disaster at Roosevelt Ranch

Heartbreak at Roosevelt Ranch

Collision at Roosevelt Ranch

Regret at Roosevelt Ranch

Desire at Roosevelt Ranch

Phoenix Series (**read in order**)

Phoenix Rising

Dark Phoenix

Phoenix Freed

Phoenix: LexTal Chronicles (**rereleasing soon, stand alone, Phoenix world**)

From Ashes

To Smoke (January 25th, 2021)

In Flames

KTS Series

Fire and Ice (Hurt Anthology, stand alone)

Riding The Edge (December 7th, 2020)

Stand Alones

Someday, Maybe (YA)

ABOUT THE AUTHOR

USA Today bestselling author, Elise Faber, loves chocolate, Star Wars, Harry Potter, and hockey (the order depending on the day and how well her team -- the Sharks! -- are playing). She and her husband also play as much hockey as they can squeeze into their schedules, so much so that their typical date night is spent on the ice. Elise changes her hair color more often than some people change their socks, loves sparkly things, and is the mom to two exuberant boys. She lives in Northern California. Connect with her in her Facebook group, the Fabinators or find more information about her books at www.elisefaber.com.

facebook.com/elisefaberauthor

amazon.com/author/elisefaber

bookbub.com/profile/elise-faber

instagram.com/elisefaber

goodreads.com/elisefaber

pinterest.com/elisefaberwrite